Knife's Tell

To Derek,
Keep The Blood
Flowing
Daniel
Dark

To Deb,

Keep the food flowing

Amigo!

Knife's Tell

Daniel Dark

SEVENTH STAR PRESS

Cover art and design: Aaron Drown Design
Cover art in this book copyright © 2017 Aaron Drown Design & Seventh Star Press, LLC.

Editor: Scott Sandridge

Published by Seventh Star Press, LLC.

ISBN Number:

Seventh Star Press
www.seventhstarpress.com
info@seventhstarpress.com

Publisher's Note:
Knife's Tell is a work of fiction. All names, characters, and places are the product of the author's imagination, used in fictitious manner. Any resemblances to actual persons, places, locales, events, etc. are purely coincidental.

Printed in the United States of America

First Edition

01 January, 1889

In each persons life there is a fog. Not the mist that covers a field in the morn, but a thick blinding dark grayness that chills your bones in dampness. I have lived most of my days in that fog, as fear encapsulated me each day. Oh but at night — that night when the real fog comes out, and I put fear aside. I fear nothing in the dark in the shadows of the park. Its steeple so high makes everyone so shy with shadows that cry. The ladies are out, looking for company, and a light, as fine gents hide in shame, less someone know their name. To be seen in these hours with such delicate flowers, would never be right of men with such might.

Each and all pass me — without notice, no eye contact, no word, no understanding. The next morning they would dread, at what horror they read. Will it lead to them, did someone see, the actions of their deeds? When they had a carnal spree with that name they see.

1 March, 1888

pigeon cooed me awake from the window seal. The little bastard suddenly realized its mistake as it prepared to be my breakfast. A quick shave with my razor will remove any unwanted head, and let me get your bath ready. A nice pot of boiling water will get you clean all over, no more of those nasty feathers. You will not need these feet any more as you lay flopping on the floor. Besides, they will be so handy to pick you out of my teeth. You made such a wonderful breakfast consisting of roasted pigeon, egg sauce, toast points, and tea. Thank you for your contribution.

As I penetrated the city, a toper from the Reform Club requested I meet him for lunch as he had something intimate to address. Reluctantly, I accepted his invitation and continued my wanderings. There is so much to observe in the forenoon. Gentlewomen in the market loading down their housemaids with goods for the day. Gentlemen rushing through streets trying to be different while being the same.

We met graciously at the appointed time in the spacious dining area. Being the babbling idiot he is, his mind as normal was awkward with preconceived thought. The words not of good recognition to his tongue. This was helped none by his drinking of strong ale. The waiter arrived, took our orders, and returned to the kitchen. There was nothing anew that his ramblings told me, but at least I had time to eat.

Tonight I found the streets delightful and robust with possibilities. One bawdy whore after another tried to coax me in with a view of their tits, or lifting and rubbing under their skirts. Showing me the goods a few pennies would fetch. I knew any of these bitches could be had for a half penny. After several hours wandering I took up my normal room at the club. The soft down mattress was always a comfort to rest a weary body huddled with a bottle of laudanum.

2 March, 1888

Aroused early in this morning, a hard knock at the door from a frantic father to be made me curse him and my chosen profession. We immediately went to the street and caught a cab to the man's house. The lady, which he knew was in labor, lay on a filthy iron bed, in a fifth floor tenement. The damned place smelled of rotting meat sat out on a small drop leaf, and excrement where she had shat herself in the bed permeated the room. Piss and water dripping through the worn out mattress pooled on the floor under her. Never less, we brought another fine son into the world. Not that this worthless clowes couldn't afford to feed it. Packing up my bag the jackass paid me in soiled doilies. What the hell am I going to do with soiled doilies?

I hailed the cab back to the club where I found Charles sitting in the library and had a literary talk about his Bleak House till dawn. We adjourned to the dining room to revivify our puissance. I was to have a rendezvous with my wife later, and asked the chef what he should bring. The chef never being one to allow dissatisfaction brought out a tray with two plates of Oysters a la Hollandaise, Eggs Molded a la Bedford in Cocottes, and Turkish Coffee letting me know of the aphrodisiac properties.

With breakfast concluded I decided to walk over to the square, and sit with a cigar. Our talk picked up where we left off:

Deciphering about the more than two hundred killed in a Moradabad district of Delhi hail storm a few days earlier.

How it was that God could kill hundreds, if not thousands, but if we killed one we would be murders.

What we thought the best methods would be to keep one from being caught, if we did commit such a deed.

His idea was to weight the body and put it in a lye pond. Mine was to make the crime so horrific that the normal man could not conceive the act. We bantered back and forth without a conclusion. Around two, I bid Charles farewell with much confusion in my mind. Another snort of laudanum was just what I ordered.

I went to the park. Meeting with Elizabeth, as our consent about the upcoming gaiety of our son's second birthday this Friday. Sitting, enjoying tea and queen cakes on a bench between the stones and statues. She expanded on and on about what the party should be and who was invited. Most of all, how I needed to be there before the guests.

The soiree was to begin at seven, as in some of the guests would need time to get there. Most of the men I knew from the club, some of which were the best orators of the theatre. Thusly, she asked me to have the invitations done and delivered by dark. Being only a little after three, I set out to the club to procure stationary and wax. I knew most of our guests would show, or already be there in the library. I myself was in want for another cigar and a Blackthorne.

I met with the appointed men and was assured that they would be able to attend. We sat and discussed the affairs of state, and how we would correct the problems. We had more to drink before some of us went on an excursion of the Chapel. I met a young lady that had desire for cash, and we worked an agreement. Tonight I spent at the club, as I smelled from the whore, and it was too late for home.

3 March, 1888

I woke with a burning in my brain and a haze of the night. I had but two appointments at the office in the mid afternoon but left the club after only some coffee. I needed to walk to discover what the night before had held. Finding no word of improper timing, I went on to the office to prepare the tinctures that I would need that day. At a quarter to one the first lady came for her appointment. The second one would be along shortly. New mothers both, the dolts understood very little of what I told them but had no questions. Frustrating. Very frustrating.

I had made myself a vial of laudanum before my appointments, and had taken three doses. Now I was ready for the outside again. The atmosphere wafted as the air perspired from the ocean winds. There would be a storm tonight. One that would keep the best in and the worst out in search of an easy score. I knew tonight would be a great victory, or death, for me as I planned the route. Where would be my refuge? Where will the rouges do their work? Perchance I flow with them ostensible while they be hoodwinked by adulteration? To study the blood flow of night like I have the body.

I needed sustenance were I to drift the streets this night. I could hear a loud pub from around the corner and ducked in for a pint.

The pub was busy with labor. Street urchins scuttled

through the crowd in exploration of a bobble they could pry. My fixation was on one such child, her eyes wide with anticipation. A purse was slung low on the well groomed gentleman to her right. With a slip of her knife she slid it into her hand and then under her skirt. He knew nothing till he was asked to pay. Mistakenly he accused the grubby laborer to his left. A short stout fellow, with calloused hands, wearing a bowler and oil leather overcoat. Following the men out to the street was the real joy of my day. Not only was the gentleman ill-suited for this type of event, but the accused was from this block and accustomed to this pleasure. The gentleman's brass-handled day stick being no match to the skill, and rib club, produced by the other. Smiling wickedly the laborer worked quickly, savagely, with such brutality, laughing continually, as he danced around his rotund accuser. Crunching of bones could be heard above the wagons and hawkers on the cobble. In few minutes the ordeal was appropriated. Intoxication of savage blood overwhelmed my spirit as I walked over to the laborer, raised his hand in victory, inviting him in for some ribs and a pint. The crowd around us clapped him on the shoulder, as we went back in. Looking him over I versed my mind in contemplation of the night.

Twilight came early tonight while the storm bellowed into view. I found myself wrought in cold fire from the sky. Energy igniting the shadows ushered in through blazing flashes within the dome of heaven. My animal instinct was awakened within, and could not be denounced. The pleasure of blood lashed out in me as I severed the head of a rat within the grasp of my cane. Crimson encased the paving as a coverlet on the bed while it crumbled, twitching, overwhelmed by what had happened. As I tired of this, a mongrel lavished at the morsel running wildly, as all do in this place when worried about capture. I'm sure this will not be the last with him. Only the shadows would be safe at this hour. Dawn would be breaking before I made it out safe. Brazenly I worked my way back past the haunts of this night to the bed that was waiting unruffled to my late arrival. I took a dose of laudanum, dreaming of a pale night to rise.

4 March, 1888

I curiously watched the back of my eyelids as the show progressed within my mind. Had I seen a woman being raped by, or raping, the man she was with last night, their moans still echoing on the stones? I was sure of it.

Today was the time for my son's event, and I needed to make sure the housekeeper was prepared. Guests would be here at 7:00 this evening, and the production must be in order. Luck smiled on me today, as she had been up early to the market and was in preparation of dinner, as well as having me a moderate breakfast at the table. She had been instructed by Elizabeth before she left to make sure that I ate. Breakfast was adequate for the walk to the office where I found a new presumed patient awaiting my arrival by the door. On first inspection I was aware of her lack of capital and invited her inside. She was young, lovely, and on her own in need of a governor to reside with. I explained my needs, and the needs of my house, sending her with a letter to my housekeeper for proper management.

When I returned home it was ablaze from within by the oil lights and candles. Upon entry I was bewildered by the sights of flowers and décor. The child was a savant of flowers, and garden, turning the whole inside into a paradise. The guests of tonight would be delighted, as I was myself. Margaret handed me the menu for my approval.

Menu
Huitres Marinees.

Potages.
Consomme Deslignac.
Cream d'Asperges

Hos-D'Oeuvre
Timbales a la Mentana

Poisson.
Saumon sauce Crevettes.
Pommes a l'Anglaise

Releves.
Felet de boeuf a la Chevrelat.
Tomates Farcies

Entrees.
Chapons a la Lyonnaise
Petets Pois au Beurre
Croquettes de Homard a la Victoria

Sorbet Regence.

Rot.
Becassines Bardees
Salade de Laitue.

Entremets De Douceur
Savarin aux Cerises.
Glaces Napolitaine.
Fruits.
Petits fours
Cafe

The menu was a wonderment to me, as I hoped that it would be to our guest. Giving the staff a few last orders, I went straight up to get ready for a night as host.

Knowing all the festivity would be counting on me.

The guest, all dead writers that almost no one had read in over a decade, ELIZABETH'S brilliant idea (the sisters Anne, Charlotte, and Emily Bronte invited by my wife, and William Thackeray, John Keble, and John Stuart Mill from the club), were right on time, as was appropriate. I was sure that Emily, thinking herself a female Dickens, would insist on doing a reading, and if that happened Lord help us. Thackeray got started. Being all of the knowledge realm in literature, at least there would be easy conversation.

As a gift I had found my son an extraordinary automaton of a lady playing the piano for his birthday and gave it to him right before dinner was served. He went to bed early after a long watching of the automaton while laughing with glee.

The party was delightful with talk, and readings from the Bronte sisters till Thackeray started. Hell I thought that the blowhard would never be quite. It was about two when everyone left, and Elizabeth came in to tell me good night. I sat contemplating the night's events, and found it was soon becoming light outside.

5 March, 1888

The fragrance of the freshly oiled walnut was a quick reminder I was in my bed. Obtaining the flask of laudanum from the inside pocket of my waistcoat, I took two healthy swigs, sitting on the edge of the bed as the warmth rushed through me. Pulling aside the drapes, the yard and streets were veiled in mist from the light rains of early morning. My mind flooded with thoughts of the night before. One person I wanted there the most was unable to attend. Although Charles had sent a message of regret, being his reading had to take him in other directions. I decided then that a trip to check on our dear friend Wilkie was in order for the day, his health failing more each day. Our delicious talk would be limited at best. Getting dressed made it less than substantial an understanding of Wilkie's distress in life.

Approaching the stairs I found Elizabeth where I expected, sitting at her writing desk, scripting notes of thank you in her flourished pen to all of our guest. She looked beautiful in the muted light from the window. I Rapped gently on the door so as not to startle her. She looked up and waved me to her side. One kiss from her and my pains dissipated like the mist in sunshine. My love for this blessed creature was more than I could describe. Even when borrowing from my friend, De Balzac "It is a beautiful plant growing from year to year in the heart, ever extending its palms and branches, doubling every season its glorious clusters and perfumes; and, my dear life, tell me, repeat to me always, that nothing will bruise its bark or its delicate leaves, that it will grow larger in both our hearts, loved, free, watched over, like a life within our life..." the words are not great enough.

Holding her hand, I led her down the arced stairs, stopping at the bottom to behold the view that was her. Light danced on her face from the prisms in the foyer transoms, fleeting into rainbows as it touched her porcelain skin. The dining room, still disheveled, lay waiting to be plucked. We packed a basket of morsels while sending our man for a cab. We were to take a picnic in the park between the stones.

Twenty minutes later our cab was there, a black and mahogany brougham with polished brass and two matching black steeds with white stockings and blaze cresting their heads in regality. The coachman leaped from the seat as the driver pulled up, immediately at the ready with door open, waiting to help us in. Taking the basket, he placed it in a storage bin under the back of the coach. The coach was appointed in purple and gold satin. The coachman was professional, and this box showed his concern for his guest. Beautiful cut flowers in crystal vase sconces, fine French wine, and brandy from de Nancy for the taking. He knew the roads well. The ride was easy and smooth, where we could talk in hush till arriving at our destination. Far too soon the outside quit moving. The coachman opened the door and step for our regress of this chamber of pleasure.

The park was almost devoid of people. As we entered through the gates, basket in tow, we made it to our favorite bench. Our son being at home now, we sat looking out over the water spending away hours in talk and wine. Knowing the world had stopped just for us and this time. How so many show envy with me for having what they may on no occasion find. I myself grateful for what I was given. Clouds billowed in across the sky, making shapes that we laughed at to each other.

As their color started changing, I took her back to the cab, confirming my love and said my farewell for the time.

I walked on to the club to pick up some cigars and a good cognac to take to Wilkie. Approaching the door of my friend, I wondered what his condition would be today. To my surprise he answered the door himself, as I was about to grab the brass knocker, greeting me with a big hug. He Admitted he had seen me walking from down the road and was waiting till I reached to knock, to swing open the door as a startle to me. It had worked as planned, and he beamed in satisfaction. I queried about his health, and as usual he waved it aside with a grin, glancing at the bottle under my arm. As I Intuitively drew the cigars from my waistcoat, his eyes broadened.

Wilkie was in a reminiscent mood talking about days, and events, of the sixties. Talking about the approbation of one of my old teachers, Sir Thomas Watson, to Baronet. Our first meeting that same year when I was still in school, and he was much younger. The Prussian festival of victory at Berlin. The visit of the Prince and Princess of Wales to Dunrobin Castle. The great plays that he use to collaborate, and perform in, with Charles. He seemed so jubilant at these memories especially, when he talked of the theaters like Holborn, with their grandeur and audiences. As the cigars burned low, and the cognac took affect on him, the tone changed to one of remorse, as I bid farewell to my sullen friend. Darkness was descending, as I made way to a hall, for another glass, and some mutton and mash.

Crowded and clamorous the hall met with my needs. Vulgarity being it's main stay of clients. I could feel myself being viewed from the dark corners. Showing the edge of my blade, as I cut the mutton turned those eyes to others less adept. The flowers waltzed through this forest spreading pollen upon many swollen stamen, gathering pennies, as token of kindness. How easy it would be to pluck a flower from this field, so a gardener could plant it in the park.

The street lamps flared wildly in the mist, showing yellow orbs in the air, as I tried calling a cab to take me home. Prospects were void of finding one. My only resolution walking the streets till I found a landmark. Being lost in these alleys of darkness, I knew I was not alone. Shadows moved slowly in my wake, ever circling closer to their meal. Clutching the handle of my cane, I released the blade, plunging it through the neck of the closest shadow. The gurgled scream filled my ears, as my punishing smile filled his eyes. Peering over his shoulder, I let him crash to the flagstone, as another shadow flashed of polished iron and brass. Exposed to the open, it was little more than a boy. A raged wildness stoked in his eyes while he watched his master die. Charging me, his fate would be the same. Yet he collapsed in tears. Cognizant of his future hopes. Patting him on the head, I knelt and placed some coppers in his hand. Telling him to get up out of the street, I grabbed his arm, hefting him to his feet. Fighting wild, he soon relinquished, following me home like a lost pup.

6 March, 1888

Fronting the windows to the street, knowing the reward of generosity, the boy would be sitting and waiting. Had I done wrong by sparing his life? This must go away. I must converse with Edgar about the local position of this street urchin. Calling him to the porch, I brought him in for breakfast of Scotch Rare-Bit and Overturned Eggs.

He devoured the food set before him in lost abandon, not looking up, except from fear it would be taken from him. As if a feral animal, his eyes always darting his surroundings, for any movement of threat. Watching him, I knew I must keep him as a pet, learn his instincts, adopting them as mine. What was his diversion? Who or what had taught him this wildness, this survival of life? His father or guardian, his lack, or plain fear? No matter, his life was about to change yet in another direction. Taking him to the cellar, I showed him his chore for what he had eaten. Leaving him there, and locking the door behind, consumed in dark shadows, he was as I found him.

When returning home I stopped to acquire new attire for my accepted charge. I was going to reform him. His fire was deep, and my desire to develop it was unquenchable. I had seen hundreds in the orphanage, that would soon be out on the streets as a menace. This one I had a chance, to nurture, to restore, to train. What was his potential, where was his higher calling to lead him? This would fall on me now, and I had to control my impulse to end it. How would I stand up to myself? I had to make him my apprentice.

Coming to the house I noticed a pair of eyes watching, waiting for me, from the small barred cellar window. Directly I went to the cellar door, listening for him. What would be his repose after being locked behind this door all day. I waited, staring at the door. Fumbling the key from my pocket, and sliding it into the lock, I released the mechanism letting the door glide open. He stood there in all his dignified dirty glory. He proceeded to tell me that he had finished his assignment, asking what else I needed from him. He flinched, as I reached out my hand to him. A smile was all it took. Kindness was all he wanted, all he needed, and what he desired more than life, but he didn't know how to accept it.

Placing him and the clothes in the housekeeper's hands, I sent them to the bed chambers for a bath, with orders for him to come see me afterward in my study. Tonight I would find the scope of him as an apprentice. He understood common orders, but could he read the text that I had privilege to acquire? Soon there was a simple rap at the door. He was here, and maybe, just maybe, to be my greatest accomplishment to date. The door creaked open just slightly as a small voice debated itself for admission. Prior to another word I commanded him to enter and stand present for my inspection. He was a good specimen of a boy, now ready for presentation. Seeing the pleasure in my eyes, a smile broadened his face, bringing me almost to laughter. Now was the time for us both to get a morsel or two from the kitchen. Cook sent out two bowls of steaming hot soup with Savant. She would be in charge of teaching him how to eat correctly at a table, beginning now with this soup.

In Savant's simple manner she informed him thusly, reading to him from a book she had, *Ladies' and Gentlemens' Complete Etiquette by Mrs. E. B. Duffey 1877*: "Soup is the first course. All should accept it even if they let it remain untouched, because it is better to make a pretence of eating until the next course is served than to sit waiting or to compel the servants to serve one before the rest. Soup should be eaten with the side of the spoon, not from the point, and there should be no noise of sipping while eating it. It should not be called for a second time."

Lessons have to be practiced, to make it understood. This one took many ventures, while bowls of cold soup were poured out, and new ones refreshed our table. I could see that a mistress would need to be commissioned. Attainment would have to wait till morn.

7 March, 1888

Having sent my man early this morning to a known house of mistresses with my needs,one was hired and should arrive shortly.

Hearing the coachman's call to the horses, I walked to the window for a viewing of my newest hire. My second was at the gate waiting, step in hand, to assist in her departure from the box. In an instant she emerged, her dress was day elegant. In a high collar button up bodice top, with ruffles around the scalloped hem, and round the collar down into a V, at the top of her breast. Well manicured cuffs with four button sergeants around them. Her skirt made of the same linen, ran to the ground, bustled, with four inch ruffles wrapping the whole of it, to a pleated hem at the floor. Her hair was dark brown in curls along the face, pulled back into braids high on the crown, and flowing long down her back. She traversed the walk to the house with grace of a poem, stepping lightly on each note, as not to harm it. Her skin was as alabaster, carved smooth by the hand of a master, without flaw to her beauty. I wanted to bed her right there on the walk.

Composing myself—I greeted her at the front door, with her soon to be student in tow. Offering her refuge in the study where we could talk, I sent Savant to the kitchen for tea and cakes. Learning that her name was Narcissa au Consort that had been taught at Cheltenham

Ladies' College. She had studied the languages of French, Italian, German, Latin, and Spanish so as to translate or teach. She had also excelled in math, the sciences, and etiquette, ranking in the top five percent of her class. I was looking over her references when Savant entered with a tray and Narcissa rose to meet her. Impressive, very impressive was her ease of use, the manners she had so well established into her life, exploded into reality. Her references were of frank response, and composed of obligatory response, to her resplendent control of duties.

I felt well of leaving the boy in her capable hands and headed off for a brisk walk to the office, and then to the club, for dissension and banter with comrades. What would be the topics today: Parliamentary procedures, economic struggle of the poor, best business practices, or the best way to break a stallion to harness? Never mind what it would be, it would divert me till my nightly outing. Walking as I was, my mind and hunger turned to the unusual that amuse, at so many of the Coffee houses. Today was to be a glorious day, turning the corner a house attendant was placing out the plaque that read, today special Blackbird Pie. Calling to me greedily, I stood at the marble top oak bar, and ordered two servings.

Leaning against the bar, I overheard gentlemen talking about a man found dead, laying in the streets. The report one man announced was he had had his throat pierced with a long blade from the front. The blade had apparently severed his spine, and then ripped out sideways most malicious. The mans head laying oblique to the body when he was found. The proprietor rebuked them not to talk about such things while he was serving food. Disconcerted, they went on to a new topic of less interest to me, and gave time to survey the whole place. The bar worn utterly smooth, with hands and coats, had stood the test with only minor signs of repair. The walls likewise echoed the depression as high as a mans' shoulder in the smoke stained wood. The barmaid slouched between men, as they groped and laughed at her sham drunkenness. Pulling away, but not quite, she cleaved to the sound of coins in their purses. Who would be her master this day? How many coins could she draw from each of them, prior to this games end? These Heathens of the flesh so unknown, would soon devour what coins they had, and their muse would be gone.

The fragrances of tobacco, mixed with meat being smoked in the place, developed an intoxication to my senses. I felt a hand casually reach past my coat to my waistcoat. Clutching hold of the small wrist, as my watch just left its secure in the pocket. The gamin convulsed to the vice upon its wrist, pleading for clemency. The soft brown eyes swelling with tears, as I turned to face them. Knowing that this lass would bilk me for all I possessed if allowed, not willing to give up on the prize, I grabbed my watch and chain, slowly releasing her with a silent warning not to run. Standing before me now, I could see the shallows of her body, as one that had missed too many meals. Pulling a coin from an inside purse, I placed it in her shaking hand. Looking up at me, uncertain as to what I wanted, I waved her to go. She finally spoke to me, so inaudible, a mouse would have to strain to hear her. The one item I did get was, thank ya governor, in her shaking voice.

Not in want of wasted time, I headed to my next challenge. The Chapel simmered with prevision as the clouds rolled back to the sea. The moon gleamed its shadows in every corner, witness to the slaughter of morality it would consume. Sculptures made of flesh were my quest for tonight in the Chapel. I found it no great task to relish the visions of carnal knowledge put before me this night. Men fucking with prostitutes of every age and sex, in every dark alley or stoop available to them. For what; a coin, a trinket of some kind? I wish I could do away with it all sometimes. Would any of these children miss their life so much? They are simply prey to the scavengers. To be devoured till they are no longer any good to them. Then thrown out into the streets for good. It would take nothing to end their pain.

8 March, 1888

detective arrived with another order from our great Frederick Abberline requiring my skills as a medical examiner. A man had been found in Spitalfields, head and body dissevered. Now would be my job to tell them how he died. Abstaining from seeing him, I would say he died from drunkenness. Retrieving this thought from my mouth, I asked for a moment to get ready. He had the police wagon setting ready to hurry us to the station. The stone garrison, a grey behemoth, shook internally with this knowledge of murder, its intestines already regurgitating rumors even before I walked through the large oak door, each one of these germs already having suspects to the crime. I was once again escorted to the door of Abberline's office. Abberline, standing stolid behind his desk staring at the papers in his hand, immediately motioning for me to enter when the escort announced me. He was perplexed by this case. In a part of town that a body normally would be stripped of any value, not an item was removed. The report showed that it should have been noticed before it had. None in the area had heard a sound, and the wound was done in one motion. The problem was that this report could not clarify if the assailant was left or right handed. This was where my implement of decree would demand further study. Eyeing the body from the door, I knew exactly how he was killed. The study of his body would still be obligatory by me. The normal assistant would not be desired except for dictation of notes. The wound had passed through the trachea and esophagus, passing between the vertebra in the neck, severing the spinal cord, scraping the mandible, and finally exiting by means of the platysma, sterno-cleido-mastoideus, trapezius, and external jugular vein. The upward sweep of the cut could have been made, from the front by a right handed person, or from behind. Holding the instrument in the left hand forward grip the traducer could come up from behind quickly grabbing the mark around the forehead, plunging the blade into the front of the neck and ripping it out sideways. I had seen this type of wound inflicted by several known butchers. It was a common cut inflicted upon sheep, to fatally wound them before hanging. This was the emphasis of my report. Abberline the skeptic greedily drew in the information that I had offered him. After a brief congress, with two of his best detectives, he sent for my escort to return me home. While I left, his orders boomed throughout the precinct, so as none misunderstood his intent. I broke a slight smile as the rain introduced itself.

The rain had muddled the streets, and the mood of those out. Everything falling into a grayness with the murky water running the gutters. Reminding me of small potatoes, running around a collection, of beef and bones simmering in broth. The house coming into view was a refuge to this day.

Arriving I was greeted by the boy and Narcissa at study in the dining room. After gleaning their source of academic and progress, I retired to my study. I would not be leaving again today, I was in need of tincture and rest.

9 March, 1888

Narcissa met me soon as I emerged from the morning staff meeting. Questions were commanding her to request that she take the boy out for assessment of eloquence. Studying her face for a moment, I granted the request with specifications and limitations, directing my man to go with them. Having had little to eat the day before, I bid Cook into bringing me a sumptuous breakfast. In short order she returned with fried ham and eggs instead.

Today secured itself with a bright sun lighting up the distance of clouds. Beams illuminated the hills where the river flowed to the city, causing the ground to blaze with colors. I needed to get out, and a short walk of ten to twelve kilometers would be good in the brisk air. Sampling the country side this morning was a wonderful choice. Coming over a hill to where a branch ran across a meadow, I spied movement at the waters edge. At that moment a beautiful lass with dark auburn hair stood up from the waters. Her hair and skin taut in cool awakening, radiating in jeweled supremacy. Sun beams danced upon her nude body, malleable and changing, as a ballet conducted by a great master. Movements within air and earth would not have shook me more. Who was she, where had she come from, alone in this countryside? My answers would not be conformed today. She ran as a faun when an errant shot is fired, with the glimpse of me on the horizon. The rest of today my thoughts have rested upon that image. I must find her again.

10 March, 1888

Looking for a report from Narcissa, I asked Savant to bring her to my study, as she was the first I had seen this morning. Moments later the knock came at the door as Narcissa asked permission to enter. As she entered, I asked her what had happened the day before. Even though I had already gotten a dialogue from my house man, Howard. She admitted that the day was somewhat deplorable, even if there were signs of improvement. The boy reverted to his former self on a many occasion, and it was normally when with people of authority. Knowing where the boy had transpired from, it would be somewhat understood. He had been mistreated by almost everyone that had dominion over him. Fear would be a great issue to overcome. Today, I would take the two of them with me, on my walk to the marketplace. He would see that the normal person would be of no concern to him, if he walked in confidence. People that knew my standings in the community would show him respect, by being associated with me. Confidence was to be an emphasis of this exercise. To show him how to exude himself without being arrogant would do great service to him, and in return to me.

I impressed that he not to speak unless I instructed him to, no matter what was asked him. Since we left before eating, it would also be an experiment in will. Would his will to do as commanded, overcome his hunger?

With where we were headed, it would be a challenge to him. I would not iron fist him like his previous master, but teach, instruct, and show him how to be proper in public. We would stand back and watch Narcissa as she went throughout the market. I knew he would have no problem with this, as his eyes were already transfixed on her. She was wearing a two piece dress. The bodice of blue silk crepe de chine, with large gold tone rose print, and blue velvet trim. Her skirt was in ivory silk, with a blue velvet inlay. Such a beauty, I found myself staring. Adverting my eyes less she see inside my mind.

"What are her interactions to show me?" He asked. "How can I learn from just watching her?"

"Observe, watch with connection to the scene being played out for you. Watching, and listening, you will learn much more than talking. I want you to watch with your ears, as well as your eyes."

He looked at me confused, but soon he was caught in her delicate voice, as well as her beauty. With each syllable she spoke, he was more and more under the spell of her words. It was as if watching her coax a bird to her from it's perch. I also wondered if it was as unequivocal in my eyes as well. This child enraptured all in her presence. She was certainly instructed by masters of the subjects that would make men falter. What would keep this boy from not falling in love with his teacher? Even I found her ways intoxicating.

Her first target was the Butcher, his cart hung heavy with cured meats. She knew his best cuts would be pilfered early. Cook had given her a list, and this morning task was to find a nice beef tongue, liver, duck breast, and rib crown. The Butcher smiled showing a row of blackened teeth. He proceeded to find her what she asked for, assuming he could take advantage of such a delicate flower. He was wrong! She had watched him as he picked the less of his products for her. On presentation and ask, she rejected it all, and controlled him to which cuts she wanted, and what she would pay. His objections only made it worse, as she told him, loud enough for passer to hear, how he had tried to swindle her. He coward to her dominance, and we left with extra for her troubles. The rest of the list consisted of assorted vegetables, soaps, and teas. Thus showing our young student her many coercive ways.

Excruciating over the loss of yesterday's vision not being found, inquiries to vendors provided me with lethal substance. Finding that she is the great niece of a lord living on the country estate, Hedsor House, in Buckinghamshire, Northwest of London, I spent the rest of the day devising a plan to get invited to the estate.

Tonight the club was consumed with extravagance as I walked in. What had been stated as a simple affair had been heightened to recreate one of Chef Soyer's grand banquettes. Chef had provided more courses than one should be allowed to eat. Eat we did, till up into the night.

11 March, 1888

My bed served me brilliantly last night. Engulfing my body in a cloud of soft feathers, where I slept off the perilous journey as a gourmand. Why had I even tried to eat it all? Knowing, that my constitution would regret the cutting of spice, as well as the massive amount of courses.

In a game of chance last night, I had obtained box tickets for the West End theatre tonight to see Marie Lloyd. Longing to bring a smile to Elizabeth, I presented her the tickets. She did smile briefly, but her pains were back, and she asked me to take Savant instead. I saw that her mind was not to be challenged and called for Savant to meet me in my study. Kissing Elizabeth on the forehead, I went to my study. Sitting at my desk, writing long overdue thank you letters for my son's birthday party, there came a soft shuffle at the door. Slowly the door cracked open, and I pressed her to come in. Considerately she asked if there was a problem with her work here. Without rising from my duty, I assured her that there was no problem except that I needed someone to escort to the theatre. Looking bewildered as to how this was to involve her, I told her she was to be my escort for the evening. Excitement blazed in her eyes upon hearing the news, as a single tear bit into her cheek. She immediately started to protest what I had said. She had heard of the theatre, but never thought that she would be going. "Why did You choose me instead of Narcissa?"

"To be honest Narcissa would have been my first, and the logical choice, but my wife wants you to be exposed to a higher class of society. Savant, you are to be employed as personal servant for Elizabeth. You should be able to appear in public events in Elizabeth's place. Tonight you are my accompany, as an escort you will be of extraordinary value this evening. Now go to Elizabeth's bedroom and find a suitable dress for this evening." Upon her leaving I returned to my letters.

After finishing the letters, and taking them to the Victoria Street post, it was time for a long walk. I entered Trafalgar Square as rain started falling, and I ducked into the club to wait it out. As normal a group had already begun to gather in the billiards room. Not wanting to get into a game I detoured into the dining hall. Finding a table near the back wall, with good lighting, and a daily news, I settled in for something to eat. Deciding on the yeast waffles with gooseberry compote, and eggs-in-the-nest.

Sitting without a time constraint, I ignored the plates delivered to my table, caught by the news of upcoming events, including the theatre tonight. My thoughts went to how Savant would be dressed, and the looks of envy on others faces, as I entertained her there.

Upon leaving the club, rain was still coming down hard. The walk would have to wait. Coaches were lined up on the square. Seeing a nice English, I haled it to the door, wanting the window view it offered. A small door opened as the driver asked where to. Giving him the address, I settled in for the ride, glad not to walk in this weather. As the coach left the square, the bells started to chime in the distance. Counting the tones it was eleven, and it would chime several more times, before Savant would hear them tonight. Wonderment would surely be in her eyes from the excitement she would witness. For now going to the office and collecting any messages was foremost. The carriage stopped with a command from above.

"Do you need me to wait for you, governor?"

With a quick yes, I made a run for the door, leaving the shelter of leather and silk behind. Stepping from the English made it desirous to have one. The extra windows made it seem like one was riding in an open top, without being in full view, of the boor on the streets.

Placing the large brass key into the lock the door swung on it's hinges to the pressure. Who was here, and how had they unlocked the door? This question was answered beyond a doubt as a blue uniformed figure came into view and turned to face me. He had questions about what had been discovered in the murdered man's possessions. When they had found him there was a cudgel with iron spikes laying close to his body. It had blood all over it and would need to be tested as to human or animal. The officer was trying to place the blood, as maybe being from the one that had killed him. The test would only take a few minutes, and then I could place the blame even farther away from myself. Assuring that the blood was indeed human; the pathetic blue bottle left with his prize piece of evidence. Watching him go down the street, I obtained all the messages from the mail slot and hurried back to the carriage. Giving the driver my address, and asking him if he would be busy tonight for hire, his large smile and nod exemplified his eagerness to the job. Climbing into the seat, there came a jolt as the carriage lurched forward. Pulling the bottle from inside my coat, I took two large swigs of laudanum before corking it. Tonight was to be glorious, and I would need to be in best shape for the events.

When I Reached the house and entered the front door, Savant flitted down the stairs. She had spent all day getting ready for tonight, and could not wait to show off how pretty she was. The dress that she had found was a deep burgundy taffeta, with puff sleeves, and a large bow in the back. She had pulled her dark hair back in wide braids leaving a ringlet of curls to frame her sprite face. To finish off her child to woman muse, a touch of rouge, rose water, and berry stain on her lips.

The results was amazing, Savant had transformed with more beauty than I had ever noticed.

Going upstairs to prepare for our evening, a strange sensation of familiar recognition flashed in visions. Elizabeth running to me in our youth. My face nestled in the waves of her hair, as she kissed my neck. Tickling her, as she fled up the stairs giggling in her girlish style.

"Life memories, is that all I have left? People that I once knew, read, laughed with, and loved; are they all gone from me? A life of humdrum continuance, persevered by the duty to work, to restore my poor Elizabeth. What else should I hope for? My failure is why Elizabeth cannot... What's the use?"

Tonight will be spectacular. Savant has adorned herself in some borrowed jewels from Elizabeth's collection. I have on my black evening suit, with a blood red silk paisley waist coat, gold watch, top hat, and walking cane.

The coach arrived at six on the bell, the driver looked at us and at once jumped from his perch. Running to the back of his coach, retrieving the proper plumage for the horses, and his hat to match our attire. Being set, and to the delight of Savant, he put down the steps, and opened the door for her to enter, a helping hand extended for her need. Closing the door behind us he climbed back into the seat, and eased the horses into motion. A good champagne, brandy, and glasses set in a fold down tray to the right for our enjoyment. Roses had been placed in the bud vases on both walls.

The ride was smooth, and deliberate. Arriving to the theatre had been too short for the giggling child next to me. The ride home would need to be longer for my plans to work out. If Savant was to be dazzled this evening then everything would depend on me.

Exiting the coach in front of the West End, the crowd out front had turned to us, as people wondered as to who was coming. Journalists stood at the front entrance with pens in hand noting anyone of importance. Savant's eyes widened to take in all the drama as people ran up to pen our names. She had never seen, much less been privileged to be one, of the noted ones.

We entered the grand lobby that shone with gold statues in the gas lights. She spun around, taking time to devour each moment, burning it into her mind. The mob of guest pushed us forward into the theatre as we were escorted to our box. The box was built to sit six but tonight we would be the only ones there. Appointed in red velvet throughout, we blended into it almost unseen. As the gas lights inside went down, the orchestra started playing, and the stage lights blazed into existence. By the slowed actions of Savant, she was mesmerized. Our seats less than thirty feet above, and to the left of the stage, gave her a perfect view of the whole of it. When it was over, she stood applauding, as tears streamed down her face.

Leaving was no less a task. Weaving among people, huddled in large clumps, talking enthusiastically about the show. The driver set waiting calmly for us to exit right where we had left him. Seeing us he hurried down to make ready. Kindly asking Savant if the evening was to her satisfaction so far, and if there was anywhere else, I desired for him to take us. Telling him that it would be a good night for a ride before home. I left it to his discretion on the path we would take. He smiled, intrigued by my confidence, and said he knew just the way. I uncorked and poured two flutes of champagne. The driver did know the way taking us on a tour of the city, past the Houses of Parliament, the Palace of Westminster with its grand clock tower, and over the London Bridge. Savant had curled up under my arm, as she sipped some champagne, taking in this glorious city of London.

The ride home had been the perfect ending to this night. I helped Savant down from the carriage sending her on to the house as I finished with the driver. Presenting him a five pound note, then turning to see what had caught his attention. There was Savant turning, spinning, and dancing up the walk to the house as the champagne did it's work. Grinning myself, and thanking him for the extra care he had shown to us, he protested the amount that was given was too large. Soon he understood the appreciation, accepting the note.

Savant had reached the porch but was having trouble navigating the steps. Helping her inside, and up to the bedrooms, I went back to the study for a quick smoke before bed. Picking up a book on elocution to practice the best ways of speaking, standing, and body control in front of a group. I stood in front of the large mirror, and practiced my speech. The clock chimed once telling me morning would be upon us soon, and rest was necessary. Coming to the top of the stairs I saw my bedroom door was closed. Opening the door, candles set all around, reflecting the bed as if the stage of the theatre the sheer curtains drawn closed. A rustle of movement just behind them. Slowly parting to reveal Savant standing on her knees in the center of the bed. Her naked virginal body glistened with oil in the candle light. The jewels she had left on, seem dull next to her swelling breast. Reaching out to me she said she wanted to thank me for such a wonderful evening. Taking one more look at her, and thinking about my plans to pluck this little rose, I regretfully sent her to her room. Before leaving, she placed my hand between her legs, where I could feel her wetness there. Ring the bell if you should change your mind, she said walking down the hall. After she left, I sat in silence thinking about the possibilities, then got undressed and went to bed. My dreams would not make the experience any less tormenting to me.

12 March, 1888

avant had not come down when I left the house this morning. Collection bag over my shoulder, I retrieved my penny farthing from the carriage house. Planning a trip through the Northwest country side was always exciting to me. I had found the best herbs and medicinals in that area, as well as the auburn haired beauty. Being almost out of foxglove, lady's mantle, woodruffe, and lovage, I needed to find a supply today.

Traveling out of Kentish Town, and on to Highgate Road, I followed the Grove through Dartmouth Park and the Highgate passageway into the country side. The ride so far was exhilarating, my legs burned from the labor and energy spent so far, offering no time to stop, as my destination was still miles away. I would arrive there after lunch but before high tea and would surely not be turned away. Scouring the road side for possible harvest sites, I worried little if I found what I hunted for out here, the house would have what I needed. Exhausted, I stopped for a short time under a small grove of walnut trees. While nibbling on some Cheshire and drinking a decent Burgundy, I practiced my speech again. Noting the location of the grove on a map, I decided that these walnuts would need to be harvested, for cook to make some of her wonderful walnut catsup. Feeling a little refreshed, the ride would be more pleasurable now.

Down the valley I saw the destination. The lord was

in a field practicing his shooting. Looking up the hill, he signaled for me to stop. Dismounting, I walked down to where he was. Going over the speech while closing the gap. Asking me why I was on his land, the speech about looking for herbs for my doctors practice tumbled out of my mouth. With an enormous smile, he invited me to the green houses. He was proud of his plants and now a doctor wanted some to make medicines. Handing the gun to a servant, he told him to tell his niece to bring tea to the Atrium for him and his new friend. We wandered through the plants for a time, him telling me how he came to gather so many specimen, and asking me which ones I was in need of. Suddenly she came into view with the tea. The silver tray sending dappled sunlight up to her face as she walked. Forgetting the question, he introduced us. In her beauty I stumbled with my response. Trying to get back to the plants, as she left he asked "she is quite lovely is she not?"

Blushing told it all. Smiling again he continued with his questions. Asking me how much I would require, and telling me that he would make sure that I would not run out. I gave him the list of my needs at this time. He handed it over to the gardener with soft words that I could not hear. Then with a flourish, he demanded that I stay the night. We sat and talked for some time before asking me if I minded a smoke. Reaching into his coat he brandished two perfectly rolled cigars and handed me one. They were of better quality than any in West End. Placing a finger to the side of his nose he inhaled the aromas first through one side then the other. Tonight was definitely going to be different. What was behind those mischievous eyes?

Dinner tonight was muted elegance with Roebuck Fillets a la Lorenzo served with bread. My host apologized for there not being more but his cook had not been expecting guest. Assuring him that it was fine, there was plenty to eat.

After dinner the niece played the piano while singing for us. Her voice was not her strong point, but she accepted our applause the same. Learning that I was a ladies doctor, the lord asked if I could take on any more patients, as his niece did not have a doctor here. Honored at the request, we set a time for her to come for an appointment. Announcing it was time for bed, with a ring of the bell a plump young lady came in, his lordship told her to show me to my room. The room was adequate with fresh fruit set in bowls for me to indulge myself.

13 March, 1888

Waking in a strange bed, in the middle of the country side, with a naked body next to me, I searched my mind as to what had happened last night. The lord of this house had extensive knowledge of plants. I had been poisoned, but what drug had been given, and when? The body beside me was still but breathing regular. Who? And why was she in my bed? Did the lord of this house want some type of dominion over me, thinking a scandal may present it? Getting out of bed, and finding no signs of my clothes, I boldly walked out into the hall in search of what was lost. The fourth room on the left side of the hall gave me a thrill as it was the niece's. Seeing her auburn hair from behind the gossamer bed drapes put a shiver in the spine. Shifting slightly in the bed uncovered one of her firm thighs. Embarrassed at the thoughts coiling in my mind, I left the room stiffly, looking for clothes to wear. After looking throughout the remainder of rooms, I returned to the room where I had awakened. Finding the bed empty, made, and clothes hanging on the stand, set my curiosity even more. A letter set on the pillows requested to join his Lordship for breakfast in the garden. With a quick wash, and now getting dressed properly, breakfast was sure to be welcome before a ride home. Walking into the garden one was overwhelmed by the scents of roses and honeysuckles. Bees buzzed from flower to flower, working their magic on the plants. Breakfast was already set, and his Lordship sat there quietly in contemplation, a cup of tea resting in his hands. He immediately arose as I passed below the trellis. Greeting me as you would an old friend he proceeded to propose of a business agreement. Now understanding the circumstance of the bedroom, but not bringing it up, I listened as he presented the details. Knowing that a local accredited doctor using his greenhouse would be paramount, he wanted my recommendation of his plants and herbs, to attain most if not all the doctors in London to purchase his goods. In return I would get whatever was required for my practice and the escapades of last night would never be mentioned again. Shaking hands on the deal, and picking up some extra ingredients, it was time to head back to London.

With the extra bundle the ride home took longer than expected. Legs burning, back in seizures, hands shaking, as the key to the office shot the bolt back with a loud audible. I dropped the bag of herbs in the laboratory, while making the way back to my private office. A dose of laudanum would help the pains, getting me ready for my patients. Today a young bride to be is coming for confirmation before the vows. An easy, but sometimes disturbing process, with both families sitting there waiting for the results. The results today were not going to be easy. The girl admitted that she could be with child, and the boy was the father. After checking the girl to affirm her suspicion, I took an extra vile of blood for the bride, and called the young man back to the office. I explained to him the pretense of what was to happen next, so he asked if there would be any way around it. I told him that affirming an untruth would be detrimental to my practice if it was found out, but I could tell a partial truth. The girl was just conceived and not showing. No one would know that it did not happen on their wedding night. The parents were happy with my explanation, and the wedding would commence this week.

Hoping that the young couple would adhere to my instructions, I closed the front door leaving for home, almost running into a constable coming in. He had been in a tussle with a man and a knife. He needed stitches in his arm. Taking him inside to get the wound properly attended he made it clear he still had work to do and nothing for pain would be needed. After cleaning the wound, he took a few shots of whisky anyway. These blue bottles are a tough bunch even when it is not to their own good. Trying to be as gentle as possible, he was still in pain, refusing even any more whiskey.

Letting him out the front door, and locking it behind us, we went our separate ways. He still needed to finish walking his beat, and there was a certain principal to his walk. Noting that his name was never given, turning around just in time to hear his whistle blow, and off he went around the corner.

14 March, 1888

Today we will start the boy with this new name, "Hardwick." Considering "boy" to be an insult to his place in society now, and Crowley, the name his old master called him too harsh. This would be done by Narcissa teaching him formal introductions. He would be required to meet certain people, and shall find introductions the best method. Narcissa instructed him that when meeting a lady or introducing her to someone else her permission would be needed before the honors were given. They practiced with Savant for a time while I watched. Savant being slightly restless with the opaqueness of the lesson. Watching her intently, her eyes drifted to me with regularity, and finally a slight grin breached her face.

Hardwick was finding every thing about this lesson to his pleasure. Having two pretty young ladies giving their attention to him. Finding praise from his teacher while kissing her assistant's hand. For once a lady was curtsying to him, instead of yelling at him to come back with what she had just lost.

The task being bound to Narcissa, out the door I went. The herbs at my office needed to be dried properly, and tinctures would need to be made. Being low on laudanum would require me to make a tonic, as well as extraction of the opium. This could be done while the herbs were in a low oven. As prominent as the plants were in the garden, they were of exquisite quality. Their yield would be higher than any thing that had been purchased in the market of the commissioner. I would have no problem honoring the agreement with his lordship.

Finished with all the work, I yearned to go to the Chapel. The taste of peril caught in the back of my throat. There would be only one release for this consumption with fever building behind the eyes. The taste of blood waxed in recent memory, and the Chapel would give me a banquette to sanctify the thirst.

Winding amongst the locals, I transformed into another. A blade in hands not known to me tested the flesh of a pig laying next to the street. It squealed, jumping to his feet, yelling that it had been cut. Teeth shown in the moon light as a tongue wrapped around the blade. The taste of iron and salt heavy in the dark liquid. Sated for the moment, the tour continued deeper into this darkness.

15 March, 1888

I had returned to my bed last night; although, the consciousness was discerning. My laudanum intake had increased to a new level, needing more each day to sequester the pains. Finding blood on the shirt sleeve hanging over the butler in the corner threw me into new questions. Had I not noticed getting blood on it when the constable received stitches? Could it have happened last night at the pub? I have no placement for the cause.

Confused, I needed to get ready for a busy day. Checking on Hardwick's progress was first after getting cleaned up and dressed. Looking out my bedroom door Savant was oiling the banisters on the stairs. Speaking to her made her jump with a start, jerking quickly around to see who spoke. Asking her to go find Narcissa she gave me a little pout before running down the stairs in her search. In just a few minutes the two of them were at my door beaming in good cheer. Narcissa wanting to report on the great adherence that Hardwick had taken to the previous day's lesson. That having worked with him and Savant had been key to his advancement. This news was good on the ears compared to the discussions held at the club or pubs every day. Telling them thank you for their diligence a wonderful aroma wafted up the stairs from the kitchen. Grabbing one under each arm, I told them we should go see what Margaret was up to this morning. Happily we all went down to the kitchen finding the source of the fragrance.

Margaret was singing, and dancing around the kitchen. Going from cutting up vegetables on the table, to the pots bubbling on the stove. A fast stir here, and there. A taste from the spoon, and adding more salt to one of the pots. She blushed from head to toe when she noticed us standing there watching her, stopping the singing and dancing. We all encouraged her to continue. Being embarrassed, she yelled at us to get out of her kitchen. We all just stood there laughing, and begging, as she finally gave into our request.

She had apple cheesecakes in the oven, giving off the aromas of fresh warm buttered bread cooking in the middle of an orchard during cider season. We all swarmed in for a taste as soon as she pulled them from the oven.

The flavors melded together. The puff paste giving away with a crunch under the tooth, offering up the buttery apple contents.

Taken back to childhood with the first bite. Being under mother's feet, as she was working around the house. Skinning my knee, and her making it well with soft kisses. Our senses, invokes what makes us smile, and cry at the same time. Feeling a tear grasping the bottom of my eye, holding, holding then falling to the top of the table I covered it with flour dust as it landed. No one had seen me cry, and today was not going to be the time for it. Turning I left the room without a word. Being the master of this house, I need not explain to others about my comings and goings. I felt them looking my way as the door closed.

Hardwick was sitting at the table reading a book, waiting for his daily instructions. Placing a hand on his head I asked if he had learned anything the day before. Wildly he sprang into action, showing me what he had learned, and telling me all about the experience of two teachers. His expression widening, as he came right up nose to nose. Ecstatic as a young school boy after his first kiss, but what could one expect, he was a young school boy after his first kiss. As he was jumping around, up, and down, bowing to no one, tipping his hat, and reaching for the imaginary young ladies hands, as the girls walked in. He looked as if he had been shot seeing the trim of petticoats in his peripheral vision. He shot up straight, both the girls already looking at him wily. He had nowhere to go, no place to hide, as Narcissa asked "are you ready for your lessons today?" The question took him by surprise, and he stammered out a few incoherent words before shaking his head yes. The girls were about to die at his expense, but they kept it to themselves.

I Needed to get to the office for more patients than I have had all week previous, and then to the station to look about a prisoner there. My day was going to be engaging till after dark. The patients were dull: at most the normal woman problems of hysteria, or some sort of weakness given to them by God. The prisoner, though, was another story. A drunk from the night before, brought in for disorderly conduct, with a long deep slash in his upper thigh. The constable telling me that he claimed some one had cut him while he was laying down taking a nap.

After getting him to the station they had wiped off the blood and sort of dressed it, but it needed a doctors hand to it. The cut was clean, telling me the blade was very sharp that made it. I told the constable that he was probably looking at a gang. One that used knifes as their weapon of choice. He nodded then set his jaw in thinking about that possible logic. Agreeing to my conclusion he set off to gather up as many of the sort to question.

Doing what I could for the man, my duty here was done for the moment. Gathering my bag I heard the voice of Inspector Frederick Abberline hailing, "Doctor may you give a moment please?"

The word, please, put me off guard. He was never one to ask for things. He was one that commanded and expected his wishes to be carried out. Approaching his door gave a clear indication of the matter on his mind. Pined up on the wall behind him, and all over his desk, were countless pictures of different murder scenes. Death in all it's horrible magnificence, blatant for all to see set out on papers. His question was consequential, asking "do you think that we will ever be able to keep up with this?" Pointing all around himself at the few hundred photos in his office. Shaking my head, at the shear numbers, "that would be one for the city to decide. You are only allowed so many officers, and each of them can only do so much with each case. Either the city gives you permission to hire on more constables, and you make some of your best into inspectors to investigate murders, or they quit committing so many. We both know that without the first the second will never happen." He looked up at me then around the room again, nodding. Appearing that he was at a breaking point I offered him some of my laudanum to calm his mind. He needed to think about another solution to his problem. He took a long draw on the bottle, looking over at me, he took another before handing it back. It was certainly not the first time for him to taste of the tonic. Trying to smile he said, "thank you" and asked me to close the door as I left.

Entering the street there was a man on his soap box, shouting. Telling those that would listen about the state of things, and how they needed to follow his God the way he saw it in the book he held aloft. A few ladies were caught up in what he was saying, but soon a constable came out and moved him along. The events of this day were a sign to me. London was coming to a clear end of the life it had once known so well, and was waking to the callous ruff handed ways of this future. Where would the largest city in the world be in the coming decade, or century? Time knew, but it was not going to reveal it just yet.

A news boy ran past with his bundle of evening pages shouting some thing about the terrors of living in London. Stopping him with a pence to get a copy, the head lines read violence, murder, and crime. A sensationalist story by the rag, about how it was unsafe to live anywhere in the city. Although most people knew that in West End it was as safe as being in your church pew, on the most part. It also put down how bad a job the police do, and the city would be just as good without them. A caricature of a blind police man, cuffed to a light post with his stick, and crimes were right beside him, helped emphasize the remarks. Scowling over the remarks gave fuel to my thought about this free press we have. What good can be done to build up a city when tearing down the foundation of what makes the city great? This was written about men I knew well, they had been there when tragedy had fallen in my life. How was I now to see this, even if what was said had some truth to it? Had Abberline seen this ahead of asking me those questions? The city would look surly at this page, and rightfully so, although I hate to admit it. Putting Abberline's concerns away from me, I headed to the nearest pub, to deliberate with an ale, before heading home.

16 March, 1888

Abberline had entrusted me with his questions. Was it because of my brotherhood or some other reason? He had never seemed to be a friend of the brotherhood, even if he did respect my obligation and words. He himself would never give such an obligation, with exception of when in the line of police duty. We are both deferent in so many ways, although ripped from different cloths. We challenged each other on many occasion, at games of mind, and chance. In the game of life, though, I had excelled in school and money. When as children at play, I could best him most of the time. He may now be over the whole department, but until life complications had worked on me, he envied my whole existence. How could I help his troubled mind?

Before morning had raised her weary head, I knew the downpour was upon us. I had heard the monsters walking into town on legs that split the darkness, and feet of dynamite that blackened the earth with each step. There would be no need in going anywhere today. There is plenty of work I need to do here. The study needs a good looking after, there are books to put away, correspondence, and papers to write. The journal has been asking for the rest of the submitted studies to be sent to them. I could get most, if not all, of it done today, if in the right mood. Yes it needs to be done, and so it shall, then I can relax.

Working all day in the study proved rewarding. The papers to the journal will be finished in one more sitting, and all the letters that needed to go out are ready for the post tomorrow. I shall send Savant up to put the books in order. It will break some of her day from being a test subject in the laboratory of Narcissa's design. She does not seem to mind working with Hardwick, but the young boy does look at her like a cheetah does an antelope. He loves the extra attention he gets when she works with Narcissa. Ringing the study bell she came up and stood at the doorway. She had not made a sound to disturb me while I read a letter, turning her head as I clutched the old pages to my chest. When appropriate, she asked if she was the one that I had meant to call. Straightening slightly as I looked up, kindly asking her to come in, and have a seat. I smoothed out the papers that were still in my hands, and put them away. Looking she asked if anything was wrong, and could she help me in some way. Her soft quite voice invoked passions through me, long sought to be under control. In my mind's eye, I saw her naked, as she was on my bed the night we went to the theatre. Why could that vision not be released? Is she now the master and I the servant? Her hand lay on my head, as I weep in the folds of her skirt. Mind full of past thoughts and sorrows, tediously working the words from there to my mouth. The foul stench of my plagued brain spews from it's fountain through a sieve of sobs. Why, why, why I kept asking, but there could be no answer from the one holding me now. After a period I heard her voice again calming, soothing, smoothing out the corners of my heart as I had done the letter. Wiping the tears that had come, she held my face in both hands, and kissed it's red cheeks. Not able to pull away, giving into the compassion she showed to me, I embraced her amorously. Taking my hand, she led me to my room. Would I have the strength to send her away. She slipped off my coat and waist coat, hanging them on the chair in the corner. Taking off my shoes and stockings, she pulled down the basin and filled it with water to bath my feet. Her touch was extraordinary, soft yet strong, firm with caressing. My will was buckling to each and every movement. Kissing down my chest as she removed my shirts, was the catalyst. I enveloped her with my arms as she was trying to fold my shirts. They fell to the floor as I pulled her to me on the bed. Feeling my pulse race as her body pressed to mine, I knew tonight would change things, but I did not care. Tomorrow would be different anyway between us, the wind had changed.

17 March, 1888

This morning Narcissa just smiled at me as I came into the dining room. Breakfast was already on the table. Hardwick and Savant had eaten and were waiting for instructions. Hardwick's lesson was to be on listening to the conversation. He was not well educated, but being taught to listen could aid him. Having knowledge, or not, about a subject was not to be of hindrance to him. I spoke to him directly for about a minute on a medical procedure that I would have him help me with. Then I asked him to repeat what I had told him. He rambled through some of it. Although most was incorrect, his mind was sharp. Training him to use its powers would not take as long as suspected. Even though most of what he had told me was wrong, in the technical realm some of the words that he should have not known he repeated. Savant on the other hand sat there dreaming about who knows what.

Rain was still sounding on the roof, with no sign that it would let go of the sun it held as captive. Having appointments in my office, and a meeting with his lordship today at the club, the only choice was to get out in it. Having Howard the houseman bring around my small hansom, I wondered, while eating a cheese omelet, and chicken croquette with honey, what would be missing this time when I leave the office. Theft from carriages becoming common now days.

Before leaving, I told Howard to go to the market and locate a copy of Beecher's Lectures to Young Men, presenting it to Hardwick to read upon his return.

While driving to work today I decided to send a message to Wilkie Collins, Lewis Carroll, and Albert Pike to reserve a meeting with them tonight. I was thinking about writing a journal to the medical society, on the studies I had performed in dealings with police work. Each of these men were great wordsmiths in their own way and having their innate balance would insure going to print. I sent in Wilkie's message that I would pick him up personally, as he would not be able to come otherwise.

The meeting this afternoon with his lordship would bring an eminently better bargaining on my part than previous talks had. I welcomed being his advocate to the other doctors and hospitals that I was connected with. He on the other hand could not place me in the house on the day of questionable activity. No one had known of the trip made there. And why would he want to discredit his own ambassador? He approached through the billiards room, and I could tell that he was uncomfortable in such, he looked at every one with suspect. Seeing me in the library room he relaxed, coming forward to greet me in the same way as we had parted on our last talk. A bear of a man, he nearly lifted me off my feet in a hug, kissing me on both cheeks. Now who was uncomfortable, it was his tradition not mine, but I let it go. We Ordered a couple of drinks, and he furnished the cigars. We talked for about an hour before the pressing subject was broken. He had no knowledge about how to market his products to the prospective business, and was leaning heavily on me, to get the word out. This being the case, not only would I get my personal supply for free but would require a cut of the profits as well. He was enraged at first, but soon understood the amount of work on my part that it would take. In the end I got forty five percent. He wanted the money without the work, and expecting me to carry the load cost him greatly. We parted with a secure contract signed by both of us. The age of shaking hands only on such a deal was dead. I would not be defrauded again.

Picking up Wilkie was always a joy. Even in these years of his life, he still held a spark of flame in his expressions. His lordship had brought me a supply of cigars. Opening up the bundle, and handing one to Wilkie, almost brought a tear to him. He saw the quality, as he took it, and appreciated the cost of each of these sticks. Pulling up to the club I saw Lewis walking in, and Albert's Carriage was headed around the corner to the stables. This is good. Both were already here, and we could have a riotous night of it all, even with Albert in our troupe, having nothing bawdy in mind for the group. We could sway with the winds of the night, returning to our homes unscathed by our time together. Each one of these men had so much to share as literates, and they were here to challenge me. From what was my research conducted, and why is it important? Why had I decided to write the book, what was the commitment to it, and in what time did I expect to finish it? Looking at them for the first time, as dumb as a child on their first day in school, I admitted that I had no idea. Albert boomed out, "Good, now we have a place to start."

The ideas about writing poured out on me from these fountains. Ideas I had not thought of, ways of taking out the boring technical without losing content, and most important, mentors to help get it done. Talking to Wilkie on the way home, he expressed that when writing his first book he was scared to do it, but more scared to keep it inside.

18 March, 1888

oward had found a copy of the book. Hardwick was sitting in the parlor reading it, looking up at any sound or movement in the room. I gave him a one word command this morning for him to work on the rest of his life, "concentrate". Sitting on the other side of the room, staring at him, was going to make him uncomfortable but cause him to do as was told him. After about two minutes he looked up at me, and I just pointed back at the book. We repeated this several times before going in for breakfast.

Margaret had cooked some squabs, and Hardwick looked at them, questioning. "Why would anyone bother there is no meat here?" He had seen the little birds before but didn't know that you could cook and eat them. After assuring him that it would be good he cut of a small piece with his knife. Laughing at him as he slowly put it in his mouth, he looked up in surprise, almost diving into the plate, his curiosity aroused by the flavors on his tongue. Asking me what I was drinking I handed him a cup and put some of the dark liquid in it. He took a big gulp of the hot beverage, immediately spitting out what was left in his mouth.

Handing him another napkin, I told him that "I said you would like the Squab. I did not say anything about the coffee."

Looking at me with disdain, I just smiled at him in

return. Soon he returned the smile, and we had the rest of our breakfast laughing and talking. Not trying to get into what he had read so far, we talked about what ever he brought up.

The life within the house had become harmonious with each bringing their own little part. Hardwick had a rough life before now, he would learn from us all. What his lessons would be were directly related with him being entered into higher society. His existence here should bring knowledge as well as influence, to carry him through his life. It would be up to the rest of the household to give him the proper care.

Savant came in wondering what was happening, she had not seen me in this type of mood with him. I rose from my chair, and Hardwick stood up straight away to get the chair for her. Smiling at him she took the seat that he had chosen. Narcissa was working wonders with the boy, and he seemed to be adapting to the changes, too. Telling Savant to take him to buy cloths with Narcissa, I handed her ten pounds to take care of the expense. He was excited by the anticipation of the two girls being with him alone all day again. Walking out of the room I told Narcissa of the plans, and that I would be at the park visiting with Elizabeth, if she needed me. She said she understood, walking into the dining room, to prepare Hardwick for the day.

Howard sat calmly waiting for my daily appointment for him. Not needing him to drive me today, his command for the day was to go out and spend the shilling that I handed him on something for his wife Margaret. He had not bought her a present in a long time. This would do wonders for their marriage. Giving a tooth ridden smile he said thank you and followed me out the door. Before walking out the gate, I told him to take the carriage, and if he wanted to pick up a fare or two while he was out. That made him smile even more, as he ran to the stable to tack the horse.

Looking back at the house there was a raven sitting above the window of my bedroom. It cawed at the sight of me, looking for something to eat, as so many were in this festering town. Having nothing with me this day, I turned and walked on to the street. It was a lovely day for walking. There had been a light fog early, but now the sun had melted the fog into the earth. A parched breeze now blew softly to cool off the crowd. People traversed one another without a single word. Acknowledged by a simple nod, or tip of the hat, as they passed. Some stopped for extended conversations with loved ones or long lost friends. My path however led to the park where my beloved waited for my visit. She would be there already, looking for me through the crowds, not knowing the direction of my travels. The talks we have are always endearing to me, broiled in the love we once shared.

The buildings loomed up as the city came closer. Jagged forms with their spires fingering the sky. Time, and distance, would not take long now. The path would turn just inside the city, slicing a sliver off the outside edge. Heavy iron gates colliding with the street on the other side marked the entrance. Walking under the archway up the trail between the stones, I could see her sitting on our bench, next to the marble tables. She was watching out over the lake as I sneaked up behind her. My shadow gave me away before I reached her with lips so bold in public. Jumping at the site, Elizabeth turned and found me behind her. Laughing nervously at herself, she reached for my hand, asking me to come sit next to her. Kissing her forehead, and then the inside of her wrist, formed a heat in her chest making her skin flush red in the bright sun.

We sat in silence for the first time in a while. Holding each other while watching the children playing with their small sail boats on the lake. Her silence ate at me. What was she thinking about? She was always talking about something. After a period of time, she broke the silence between us. She was worried about me, but had no idea why, she just knew that some thing was different in me. Assuredly there was a difference, but I was not going to tell her about my pains, or the need for more and more laudanum to subside them. She had enough worries to tax her frailties, me adding to them would not be gentlemanly of a good husband. I did tell her of our new business partner, his Lordship, and the extra money we would earn from the sales of his cuttings, to other doctors. This seemed to please her, as more money coming into the house would do us most in this time. She decided that my extra work load was the issue. With concern in her eyes, she confessed there was nothing else she could do about it. Kissing her cheek as we parted, I told her that it would not be much longer.

Going back thru the gates, the sun just starting to set, I headed East into the city toward the Chapel.

19 March, 1888

Last night I saw the man with the knife. He was pacing around the bedroom, on the other side of the window, in the middle of my room. Blood still covered his hands, and the liston he held, dripped crimson from it's edge. He kept coming closer to me, till we were almost nose to nose, as I looked in and he looked out of the window. His eyes pierced me as he looked over his shoulder, hiding what he was doing on the small table in front of him. Time passed slowly, before he turned facing me again. Holding up a small piece of red leather for me to see, and dropping it into his mouth. Chewing it insidiously as he watched me with fascination. Hurriedly I ran to my basin to wash the sweat from my lips and hands. Turning out my lamp the room went dark and the man was gone. I knew as I stood in the dark that we were connected.

20 March, 1888

I woke with Savant sitting at the foot of my bed watching over me. The room had been cleaned, and there was fresh water in the pitcher and basin. A wet cloth was on my forehead, and a look of concern on her face. Food sat untouched on a tray next to me. She came to me as I stirred, the worry slowly melting from her face. How long had she been here? She poured some water as she asked if I was okay. Weakly I asked how long I had been asleep. Telling me that I never got up yesterday, and it was now two in the afternoon. She had been here with me since about that time the day before, waiting for me to wake. She asked if I could remember the dreams I had, that caused me to have such fits while I slept.

I did remember some about a dark alleyway, but they were too disturbing to relate to her. The man with the knife had appeared to me, laughing, as he savagely attacked a man from the pub. He plunged the knife deep into his side disemboweling him as he drew it to the other side. He then stabbed, and cut, and slashed till the man was dead. The thought of it gave me chills as sweat started pouring from my brow. Closing my eyes to it, shaking my head to relieve myself of the image.

Savant waited for me to come back to her. My eyes burned with tears as she handed me the glass of water. What could I tell her that would help? I had slept for over a day but still felt worn out, that would not do. Telling her of the dreams would be even worse. Genuinely I asked for the food.

"Who is Frederick?" Savant asked, setting the tray over my lap.

"Why? Is something wrong with him?"

"A constable came by and said that Frederick wanted to see you as soon as possible."

"He is a friend and the chief inspector for the police force." I confirmed her by letting her know that I had a working relationship with them, also Frederick and I had known each other since we were boys. I finally asked, "Did the constable say any thing else?"

"He said that it was a matter of grave importance that you come see him."

That being said I turned to the tray in front of me. Quenching my hunger quickly, I hurried to be ready for my trip to the police station.

Entering the station, a constable rushed out the door past me. I heard Frederick yelling in the back of the hallway. His voice blasted through the narrow space. I had not caught him in a good frame of mind. Which, to my understanding, was less often these days. Seeing me, he stopped yelling long enough to motion for me to go to holding. I knew he would meet me there shortly. Frederick came in exasperated at the lack of confidence in his men. Murders were piling up, and the work load of each man he had was beyond what they could do. The families of the dead were not interested in others' cases. They wanted theirs solved, and solved fast. The latest was a man found in an alley way completely eviscerated, his body laying in the back cell on a table waiting for me.

The man's intestines were piled up on the body in a heap. Multiple wounds to his chest, shoulders, and neck were apparent, without even entering the cell. The attacker had put a knife into the man's right side ripping it across his middle. Letting the intestines fall to the ground as he, or his accomplice, continued the assault. There were nine stab wounds to the upper body, and the throat had been cut from ear to ear separating his esophagus.

"Well Doc, what can you tell me?"

"Frederick: it appears to be the work of two men. One left handed and the other right, as the two main cuts started on opposite sides of the body."

He grimaced at this, and asked, "could it have any connection to the man you had examined earlier with his head almost cut off?"

"It would be a very good possibility that at least one of the assailants could be the same." Knowing in my mind's eye that it was done by the man with the knife I see in my dreams.

This being confirmed, he called one of his men and told him to round up any one left handed, of violent nature, with a knife for questioning. With out questioning, the officer grabbed a few more men on his way to the wagons. Frederick looked fragmented, as a vase that had been dropped, and not all the pieces fit back together. I could do nothing more for him except take a swig out my flask and offer some of the tonic to him. He accepted it with a pitiful smile.

"Frederick, come by my office tomorrow, so I can get you a bottle of your own."

We parted, both knowing that he would not show.

21 March, 1888

Today I got to my office early in case Frederick did come in. I had plenty of work to get done, and was not expecting any patients till noon. Normally keeping the morning hours for emergencies that had come up from the night before. As presumed, the stubborn ass did not come in. I made up a bottle of Laudanum before I went out to get some lunch at the pub around the corner, leaving a message on the door if I was needed. I would deliver the bottle to him later in the day.

I had left message with Howard before leaving this morning, to have Narcissa bring Hardwick to my office at one o'clock today. I needed to get him familiar with the lab work. Having him work hands on will teach faster than books at this critical time in his life. He needed to build confidence in his personal ability. Today he would be learning the herbs on hand, memorizing their use, and how to make the required tinctures. This will take up unto the dark hours for him to get the required knowledge of the four herbs he would be working with. Before he would ever be allowed to work with some of the collection, close supervision would be required for his safety, and that of my patients. Foxglove and Laudanum, being of the strictest receipts in my book of medicines, will be off limit to him. Although this day he would start off weighing out, and mixing herbs, for making tins of teas, and aromatics. I started him out making some mixtures for morning sickness, as he could not get the amounts wrong. Showing him what plants to use in each tin, I got out my largest mortar and pestle for him to crush the dried herbs and left him to it.

22 March, 1888

Hardwick had done exceptional in the task given to him yesterday, weighing out ingredients for almost fifty tins of each tea. The main bulk would be for different forms of sickness due to pregnancy, the others for minor stresses of the mind. Women are such frail things, the least thing shall make them weak. So few have the constitution of men. Finding such a hardy specimen will take some searching. How will I find what I need in a place like London? There has to be a way of releasing Elizabeth from her ailment. These last few years have not been kind to her. She stays in her bed, except for the days she comes up to the park, for our walks amongst the tombs.

I miss her sorely, the calling of the house removes some of my hunger, but my memories drift to her. The times we had walking the streets after the plays, searching for that special sweet pudding. The street vendors made the best, and always knew of a secluded spot that young people in love could find. She was so beautiful on stage. The men after her performance showered her with accolades, as I stood in the back watching over her. No one, once, knew she was married.

Needing to get out of my thoughts, I went to the Chapel for a day walk. Arriving about mid-day, the sun hammered the cobblestones into the streets, as they let off waves of perspiration. Finding a mead merchant set up next to a corned beef and krout cutter, my lunch was made. I found a comfortable curb stone and made myself at home.

Piercing the crowd in the street, a young girl in a dirty red dress came up to face me. Clutching a frozen faced porcelain doll to her chest. It's blue eyes matching the child's, stared blankly into the crowd, as the child transfixed upon my food. A slight motion with the plate brought her up next to me. Her nose almost touching the edge as I placed it in her hands, and laid the doll on the curb next to me. Angrily the fork stabbed into the tin, as the small fist fought to control it. When she finished I told her to take the tin and fork back to the merchant, returning to me for a reward. She questioned my authority till I produced a half pence from my purse. Running wildly across the street, waving them in the air at the man, she pointed back to where I had been sitting. Scrutinizing the crowd, in search of me, she jumped as I touched her shoulder. Giving her back her doll, and dropping the coin in the little pocket on the front of her dress, I bid her a hearty thank you for having lunch with me, and with a deep bow asked her permission to be dismissed. Chuckling beyond her control she waved her hand as if she was the Queen. I took my leave and walked into the horde of bodies.

Not walking a block yet, I smelled a faint whiff of a din coming from a lower level window, the panes cracked and weathered. Pulling my notebook and pen, I scratched out the location for a night time visit.

23 March, 1888

hapel, oh glorious Chapel, your darkness covers, and your deeds are done in solitude.

"Give me your valuables or get your head bashed in. Your choice, but I will have them either way." Darkness concealed the gruff voice's owner. His soft leather soles made no noticeable sound before his hands were on me. The blow from his fist to the back of my head sprawled me to the ground as punches rattled ribs together. Twisting to face him I plunged the blade deep under his cage. His grip on the bare skin of my neck softened. The crunch of grizzled tissue torn apart with the twist of wrist pleasured me more the he. Blood slithered down my hand collected on the cuff before leaping to the ground in red goblets. His light was being sucked from his body, as he pleaded for help. I lowered him to the ground, the wrench that hung from his belt clung to my palm, and started beating on him. He laid there in the dark, for what seemed hours, before finally dragging himself and the wrench to the river. They both toppled in with a splash. Ripples radiated out from the wall, leaving me alone. On the other bank voices could be heard laughing and singing. The bridge was right above so why not cross and see the nightly sights before returning home.

I woke from a dream, about a party when my parents were still alive. I was in employment there, and the woman that I worked for was stern but compassionate. I had said that I wanted to get out of there to one of the girls that was working also. The building was hot in the kitchen area, and the man giving the speech was long winded. My voice carried across the room but the words were misquoted to my boss. While getting ready to serve she called me back into another room, wanting to know why I had spoke of our honored guest like such. I tried to explain that I was hot in the kitchen. I wanted to get out, not that I wanted the guest to get out. At that time my mother broke thru the door in tears. Looking for my father in a fret. Being gone so much of the time with different wars, when she could not find him, she would break down into fits of frantic. I excused myself to help her, and soon we found him outside on the veranda, smoking. Mother ran into his arms, tears damped his shoulder. My heart beat inside my head, as I watched her love for him. Knowing one day she would no longer find those arms to hold her.

24 March, 1888

A buoy was found floating in the Thames. His face, beaten and caked with blood, had been eaten by fish on the side that lay in the water. The cool damp wind and water current had shoved him under a dock, where he stayed and bloated, till two men jumped into the waters, freeing him from the cables and boards. I was called in to do the postmortem. On first exam I opened an incision in the abdominal cavity and inserted a tube for the gasses to escape. They always leave with a sinister hiss, mad at being disturbed and forced to evacuate. He appeared to be in his early thirties. Brutally built with powerful sinewy muscles. Exploring the body further there were several crescent shaped marks on the torso as well as one predominant one on the back of his neck at the base of the skull. He had been ambushed with out a doubt. Why and by whom is now the question. I called in the weathered Bobby standing outside the door to help me turn the body. Seeing one of the marks he immediately said that it looked like a large wrench to himself. Studying one of the clearest marks showed it to have been an inch and three quarter across the inside of the crescent. The bearer would have worked in a factory on heavy equipment at some time. This would not be much for the detectives to work with. Numerous factories line the river upstream from where the body was found. This would not turn up anything, as the attacker may have met a similar fate.

25 March, 1888

The body found yesterday has been identified. Yes, the one under the dock. Doran Gilpatrick, an Irish organizer living on Osborn Street.

Where he was found had very little to do with how he was found. A little girl with her doll, trying to see the fish under the dock, had peered through the cracks. Only to see two bulging eyes almost popped from their socket. Screams of terror startling the fishermen to her. They pulled her away from the trauma, as she cried mercilessly. The fishermen trying to console as they wrenched her body from the sight.

26 March, 1888

An invitation came from his lordship beseeching my attendance at a masquerade to be his niece's escort. My mind staggered back to the first time I saw her at the stream. The cascading waters made the stones sing to her beauty, as it carelessly quited in the pool where she bathed. I had stopped at that spot on each visit I made to the house. I can still see her housed in rainbows of color silhouetted against the green and gold of the grasses. There would be no doubt to my response. His lordship has knowledge of my desire for the child. Why does he play with me in such matters?

27 March, 1888

I sent my response back to his Lordship this morning, telling him I would be there. Even though I was certain he knew my answer.

There would be much to attend to before I departed, and I would need everyone in the house to be heedful to it. Howard was already in the carriage house mending the bonnet on the carriage. Margaret was packing the larder in preparation for house's needs. Narcissa had taken Hardwick with her on errands, picking up items for Margaret and myself, while Savant begged me to come back to bed. I swear she would keep me in bed all day if I let her. She is nothing more than a woman; although, I find it harder and harder to dismiss her to her room. Her lifeblood seems to envelop me when I'm with her. My desire ramping to new levels each time. Today however there was too much be be done, and I could not have her distractions. I rousted her from my bed and told her of her duties of this day. She protested with a pout, but obeyed my commands none the less.

Tonight the Chapel seemed demure in activity as I walked un-accosted through the shadows. The farther I worked my way into the heart of this place the more ominous this night felt. An old herring bone brownstone intrigued me to take a closer look. The building had once been a prominent storehouse, but now it's inhabitants were less noted. A small glow of light emitted from one of the blacked out broken windows, although no sound could be heard from within. Moving closer I knew that I was being watched. Nothing happened in this area without the knowledge of the Shadows. The Keeper's informants and henchmen would report all back to him. Abberline had told me stories of the Keeper, and his Shadows, but even the police had no idea who or what they were. Of all his stories this one intrigued me most. How could anyone control all the wickedness and immorality in this ink blot of death and debauchery? I knew at that moment that one day we would meet, if my travels kept me coming to the Chapel. As for this night I slowly backed my way out of the Chapel as the light went out from behind the window.

28 March, 1888

ast night I tried to remember every step to the brownstone. I wanted to see it in the daylight, and left for the Chapel right after a bowl of hominy porridge.

The walk was cluttered with people as they all wanted me to give or buy something, confusing my steps. I found it necessary to recount my paces on several different passages before seeing the building. Even in the daylight this place was hard. I walked in front of the building without stopping. Taking in every detail even down to the small design carved into the keystone above the main entrance, an eye with a skull in the center. The carving was not done when the building was constructed. It had to be something that dealt with the Shadows. Except for the feeling that I was being carefully watched; there was no sign of life. As the night before, no one went in or out of the building, or walked this street. I knew that there was more to this place than a tatterdemalion, and I was determined to find out. That had to wait till the night where I could be as one of the Shadows.

Today Frederick finally came in for the tonic I had carefully made for him. He told me he had been planning on it sooner, but we both knew he had been smoking his own form of medicine. I stopped long enough to energize with a cup of tea, and conversation with my friend.

29 March, 1888

Today was a busy day at the office, as I was trying to get everything possible done before leaving for Buckinghamshire. The trip would take a good portion of the day if weather permitted, and I was not going to be able to leave until Saturday late noon as it was.

To think of ones actions and words before delivery will show the manner of a man.

"Indeed, to stand composedly in the storm, amidst its rage and wildest devastations; to let it beat over you, and roar around you, and pass by you, and leave you undismayed, - this is to be a MAN."

-Lectures to Young Men : by Henry Ward Beecher 1846

30 March, 1888

In teaching Hardwick I reminded myself of why I continued my studies each day. By knowledge I can free myself of life's mundane task, increasing my own worth. This is why His Lordship has embraced me as his spokesperson to the other doctors and apothecaries in London. Today I had meetings with constituents, at the club, so as to report to His Lordship on my visit. Gathering the placement of several orders from those that I met. With special request from a few, to be able to walk his gardens and greenhouses in the near future. I set out cane in hand to have a night at the Chapel. With the moon shining bright, it gave light to those in the shadows, making concealment almost impossible. Almost being a very key word when it came to the Shadows.

31 March, 1888

I awoke early morning in the middle of a trash heap, divested of all worldly possessions. Including my boots which were a good leather and monogrammed on both sides of the uppers. I never saw who hit me or with what. They were sending me a warning that this was their part of the city, and to stay out. They had not killed me, even taking care to put me in the heap, as to not freeze, in the cold night air while almost naked. Had that order come from the Keeper? Did the Shadows do it on their own, or was someone else invoked to help me realize the dangers of this jungle? In taking my coat they took my tonic, which my body cried for with strong criticism. The walk to the Club would be humiliating, but shorter than going home, and I had fresh clothes there. To my fortune the sun had not risen, and most of the walk would be in the light of the moon instead of broad sunlight.

When the doorman saw me coming around the corner, a look of horror jumped upon him. He ran out with a long coat for me to put on. Some of my chaps were up having breakfast already, waving me over to join them. I called back to them I would shortly, but let me freshen up a bit first. With a smile and a wave I went up the side stairs.

Later on after breakfast I gave the doorman a pound note telling him the coat was in my room, and thank you for his discretion. All he said back was it was his job, and he would slip up to retrieve it later.

To my surprise the house was in a flurry getting ready for my trip. Everything was in the carriage waiting for me to be under way. The sky was clear when I climbed onto the drivers ramp and asked the horse to take on the load. The small carriage lurched forward as the Thoroughbred put its shoulders to the task, smoothing out to a gentle sway as he clopped down the road. His hooves echoed off the stones with a steady rhythm allowing my own thoughts to drift. Going straight through the city would be the shortest distance, but longer in time as well as extra stress on myself as well as the horse. I decided to go around the outskirts of the city common. This took an hour off my time, and we enjoyed the country side for the rest of the day. Arriving at the manor a little after dark Brite ran down the front stairs to greet me.

1 April, 1888

Walking out of my room there was a noise coming from Brites' room. A nickname her uncle had bestowed on her as a child, was more fitting than ever. Proceeding down the hall to the open door, I saw her laying nude, reading, on the chase in the sun light, a faint aura radiated from her. The room glowed from having all the curtains open. Sun light striking the gilding of the woodwork throughout her room. She turned to face me as her hand moved from between her thighs. A mask of black lace and feathers with small pearls threaded into the lace around her eyes failed to cover her craving. Inviting me in she stood and walked to the bed, placing the book she had been reading upon a table as she passed. Turning to close the door she asked to leave it open for the staff as they have very little to amuse them. I closed it anyway and walked over to her. She grasped the buttons on my breeches letting them fall to the floor as she knelt in front of me a hand on each hip. The down mattress on her bed enveloped us like a cloud as we lowered to heaven. Kissing me softly across my chest all the way down to my legs her eyes searching my face for just the right expression of pleasure. I pulled her lips back to mine and greedily took her body.

Yes, it happened just like that.

No, I'm not lying!

After breakfast of egg fritters we walked through

the gardens. Our bodies spent from the morning activities we stopped at one of the many benches. This was one of her favorites as the bench was a wide slab of marble supported by bronze figures of two men and women embraced in a kiss. She had led me to this one. It was in the center of the labyrinth and could not be seen from anywhere else on the property. Lifting her skirts she sat straddle of me moving her pelvis to the music coming from the house. My arousal grew as I tried to utter words. Nothing came from my lips except a deep moan. She was my siren, and she knew that I was totally in her control. Clouds came between us and the sun, casting a shadow to cover the garden, as a slow rain drenched our clothes. I was unable to stop, and she had no intension in letting me. The rain intensified my senses as the marble slab pooled with water beneath us. I felt her body contract in pulses before she fell upon me. Her breathing started to slow as the rain shower ended.

The letter that I had received, had been a fake. His lordship was not even at the house.

Away on business somewhere.

How should I know where or what his business was?

Like I was saying. The only masquerade was that of Brite's with her little lace mask that she wore all day. In her words to the honor of Fool's day and hide under it's mischief. I had enough of people hiding in cloak and shadow with the man with the knife. The morning activities had energized my blood, but had flamed pain in the rest of my body. I had tried to politely excuse myself. Brite would have none of it, she had tricked me into coming, and was not going to waste a minute of my time there. We retired back to my room where I could get the relief I needed. The bottle was hidden in a compartment of my bag. I went straight to it, taking a long pull. Brite looked on acquisitively, asking if she could have a drink. I thought that it might calm her down and handed her the bottle. She took a drink as she had seen me do and gulped it down. Within minutes to my bewilderment she was dancing around the room laughing without a stitch of clothing on. My pain beginning to subside, allowed me to join her, as she pulled me to my feet. The ardor of youth and the appetency of man can lead to an intoxicating debauchery. We made love in every room we could find. Running up and down the halls uninhibited, finally falling asleep in her bed.

2 April, 1888

I awoke in my carriage, my horse haltered and tethered to a post, my bag packed and stowed under my seat along with a basket of cheese, bread, and wine for the trip home. The house was dead silent when I pulled through the gate to the road. No one came out to see me off — not even Brite. Had his lordship come home early and found me in Brite's room? Whatever the reason I knew it was time to leave.

Passing the stream, I had no reason to stop, new memories braced me for the long ride home.

I stopped at the field of foxglove to refresh from the basket and gather herbs. Sitting next to an old stone wall I recapitulated the previous day with Brite, longing for Savant's gentle touch, to work the soreness from my limbs. She would be there when I got home.

The rest of the ride home fretted me with thoughts of the man with the knife. I had visions of him in the dreams from the night before. Had he been in the room with Brite and I? There was no way he could have been there, but the vision was so real. The knife glowed in the dim light, as the blood dripped down its edge to his cuffs.

Waiting and ready for my return, Savant ran out into the yard as I came into sight of the house, jumping onto the carriage and kissing me before I had time to stop. She had made sure that water was already on the stove waiting to be brought to my room for a bath.

Howard lugged the buckets up the stairs and poured them into the tub as he asked "How was your trip?" in his sly smile sort of way.

I smiled telling him, "It was good, and we will talk more about it tomorrow," knowing that we would not speak of it again.

With a yes govner he cut a look at me and Savant. With a knowing grin he left the room, closing the door behind him.

Savant undressed me, laying me down on the bed to work out the soreness of the ride home before helping me into the tub. As always her hands knew just the places to touch. I couldn't restrain the pleasure any more, releasing myself to her waiting mouth. Taking the girth of manhood fully in, and stroking it with her tongue made it harder than before, as she attuned her body to mine. Letting her top open, exposing the small perfect nipples to graze my thighs, as she slid up to bite softly on mine. Electricity exploding in my body with each impact of teeth to delicate flesh.

Sleep comes easy in her arms, and this night was no different.

3 April, 1888

Up early with Hardwick in the office. I hurried him into bundling and hanging the herbs collected on the ride home and from the greenhouse to dry. He needs to know how to identify them in both states fresh and dried. His education increased with Narcissa pushing him to excellence all weekend. He was able to tell me most of the fresh herbs that I brought home, and labeled them before hanging. I explained the rest to him and had him practice drawing them with a medicinal description of each for future reference. He placed his best drawings, which he had written on the back of, in a box and continued on with his work. When I left the shop he was at his desk studying Henry Gray's anatomy book, his fingers tracing the pictures as he read, looking back and forth from text to diagram making mental notes of each page.

His new introduction this week would be into Parliamentary Practice. He should be able to learn the basic rules this week. Narcissa understood some of the rules from her training; although, I would need to teach most of this to him. This knowledge would prove vitally important in his future affairs. Where better than the House for him to learn and ask questions? I made time in my calendar to take him for a late session this week.

4 April, 1888

The Man with the knife wandered my dreams last night. In the dreams I witnessed him attack a young lady on Osborn street. Not as a witness of him, but looking through his eyes as the deed was done. I could hear his words in my head as he spoke to her.

Down stairs Hardwick fervently read the book I had given him on procedures and Parliamentary practice, preparing for our outing. He knew that I was taking him to watch, and he wanted to impress me with how much he understood. Walking with a purpose beside me, he started to recite the opening procedures. I was actually amazed at what he had retained, but I didn't let it show to him, as I asked him questions I knew he could not know. Parliament opened with it's normal staunch pageantry. Hardwick was trying to look everywhere at once. The excitement he held inside, almost exploding from his body. To Hardwick's objection we left before the closing ceremony. He had scribbled notes during the political tournament. Now he poured out question after question, trying to grasp the concept of what he had seen. I worked to give him the answers, evading some altogether.

5 April, 1888

Leaving Hardwick at the office to accept appointments, I spent the day at the club in meetings. Men of high prestige joined me to discuss the plight of the East side. Each of us knew that there was no real answer to the problems of the poor. The attacks of violence had been escalating as it always does in such an environment. I never brought up the man with the knife that I had seen several times now, even though others mentioned the events. A few questioned me about the autopsy that I had done on the floater. I told them that I could not talk about it, the case was still under investigation. Most dropped it without any other questions. In the end nothing was settled.

When I returned back to the office Hardwick had sold a few tins of tea and filled my book for the rest of the week. Walking him back to the house we talked about his day and how well he was doing in his studies. He is one of he best apprentices I have ever taken under tutelage.

I left him with Savant and went back to the club.

There was a new member there, from across the pond, buying drinks for everyone. He was suppose to be a doctor, but I had my suspicion. We talked for a bit, and he didn't understand the fundamentals, that Hardwick already knew from his studies. I left and went for my nightly enjoyment in the Chapel. Elizabeth was getting worse, requiring that I get the items needed for her treatment. I believe the Chapel is the best place to retrieve those items, and I needed the Keeper to let me pass.

Being groggy, from a blow to the back of the head, I found myself being held up on each side in the dark. I was hoodwinked with a cable tow around my neck, and knew someone close had a firm hand on it. My head ached as a booming voice asked what brought me to their order again. Not knowing what to say, I simply said, I was looking for more light and hoped that the Keeper of light could help me. He said to take me back out, and soon he would inform me of his decision.

The heavy door scraped, as it took force from my escorts to open it, an ominous odor of death penetrated the hood as I was pushed through the opening and into a carriage of some type. The driver, taking little care about his passengers, lurched the horses forward before I could sit down, throwing me to the floor. He raced through the streets, hitting every hole in the road. I tried to get into a seat but was held in place by the escorts. Rough as the ride was soon I was thrown out of the door of the carriage. The hood being pulled off as I fell to the street. The carriage had never stopped. Getting to my feet and looking around I recognized the place. I was standing in front of my house. How did they know where I lived?

6 April, 1888

All I can do is wait on the Keeper to send me notice… If he does not give me pass, I will not be able to collect the items required to animate Elizabeth's health. The clouds are dark, making a meeting with her at the park wearisome if the rain comes in. The wet marble benches and stones permeate cold into the bones above and below on days like this.

Getting to my office a note on my desk caught me off guard. It only had five words on it (midnight tonight brownstone come alone), I knew the meaning and who it was from. They had left it without a trace. I had not expected the notice so soon, but was not going to miss the opportunity to talk to the Keeper in person. Hopefully?

As night fell my heart started to race with anticipation. Dropping by a pub before an excursion into the Chapel, most of its patrons huddled together in small groups, trying to talk above the other groups. Several inspected me as I came in alone. Not many walked this area without escort. The place had a heady fragrance supported with spilled ale and spittoons. Finding a open table located near the back was a good place to survey the people that were watching for easy palm. The barkeep said I needed to order something or get out. I got a pint and pie.

The wench made it to the table with the ale, and no pie. I Pointed at the end of the bar to the pie. She turned, grabbed, and slammed it down on the table. With a drunken growl she asked if there was anything else. I shook my head no, pulling out a spoon, as she went back to her drink. There were more than a few in there that would like to catch me out alone. One looking cautious at me and the door. Did he know that I worked with the police, or had been there the night Hardwick had come to live with me? Either way he was nervous about seeing me. Making a mental note of him, I gave up the table for the end of the bar and another pint. Thinking it might be better to not leave out the front door. The barkeep nodded, motioning to the curtained wall that lead to a back hallway. I Finished the ale, sitting for a while before exiting when no one seemed to be looking. The hallway went to stairs and then down to a back alley about four feet wide. Almost no light filtered into this area. Seeing a dim light at one end, I chose to go the other way.

My meeting wouldn't be for a few hours, and nothing would keep me from it. Not even the Shadows. They knew that I was to be there tonight, and imaginably had orders to keep me out. Wearing all dark clothes, the assistance of the new moon made slipping into their ranks easier this time. The Watcher greeted me warmly when he saw me standing at the end of his hall. He said most never made it this far into the inner chambers, and he would inform the Keeper shortly after my preparation. Two of the Shadows took me to an adjoining chamber and prepared me to be properly presented. Waiting seemed forever with the constant doubt that I would ever leave this place. The door opened where the two that brought me there was joined by a third armed guard. Blindfolding me as before, they conducted me to the inner chamber. Not able to see, I was ceremonially brought and formally introduced to the Keeper. Feeling the presence standing over me, his voice was kinder than expected as one question was asked. Bewilderment rushed my soul hearing the sound of others shuffling around me. The answer not coming from me but one that had brought me to this place. Others joined in as the blindfold was removed, and I was free to look upon the men. The Keeper stood directly in front of me, as a bullseye shone on him from behind obscuring any features. Reaching down he helped me back to standing while announcing me to all in attendance. The others introduced themselves one by one as the Keeper took his chair in reverance alone in the far end of the room. I had been accepted.

Wind ripped through the streets and alleyways, a coldness caused me to pull my coat tighter, bracing for the walk home.

7 April, 1888

Freedom to go anywhere in the Chapel had been granted me. Now I could search for what I sought, knowing the Shadows were in my trust.

Last night most of my tonic was used on the trip home. Putting my teeth to the cork of a new bottle, I knew the bitter taste well. Bones still aching as the man with the knife still haunted my visions. In moments both would be…

8 April, 1888

Savant sat quiet, sewing in the corner of the room. A tray of food sat next to her, prepared and ready for me if I was to wake. That would not happen this day.

9 April, 1888

Waking to the press of warm flesh, I stirred gently to face Savant, nuzzled in like a cat looking for a mouse. Her touch curious, desire unquenched in days boiled to the surface. My skin jerking impulsively with each stroke of a finger. Muscles filled with blood moved involuntary to her lips and tongue as their magik ignited flames under the skin. Spinning me onto my back she straddled my waist posting as if in a saddle. Her breast arched high toward the sky as soft moans drifted in the air. All energy seem to leave her as she collapsed upon me. Her lips next to my ear whispered for me to do as I wished. Wanting to know the power felt by the man with the knife I pulled out some silk cravats, blindfolding and lashing her to the bed, before retrieving a riding crop from the chifforobe. Kneeling over her; tracing the edges of her breast with the leather tip; bringing it down hard on her pink taunt nipples; her face contorting in pain and ecstasy she could do nothing to resist. Fighting against the restraints, begging for me, the little bitch's cunt soaking the sheets with each stroke of the whip. Ummm the feeling flooded over me as her teats swelled from the punishment drawing my mouth to the swollen buds. Pushing the blindfold aside and freeing the knots on her left hand, she immediately grabbed the back of my head, moving my lips between her thighs, as the sweet taste of her juice erupted my senses. This was my first taste of a woman; it will not be my last.

10 April, 1888

Feeling fully rested but hungry, I rushed down stairs to see what Margaret had ready for breakfast, only to find an empty kitchen with a note that there was some cold meat in the icebox. Apparently the rest of the house had gone to the market. The icebox door swung too hard as it collided with the drainboard. Several dishes crashed on the tile floor as the door latched itself again. I left them there as I walked through the house looking for someone to reprimand. First impressions had been correct as gleeful voices filled the back stairs. The glee ending as they each saw me starring into the kitchen, broken dishes scattered across the floor.

Yelling at Hardwick to go get ready as we were already late for my first appointment, the rest took flight to other parts of the house, except for Margaret that had come back with a broom and dustbin to clean up the dishes. Glaring at her for a moment let me calm down enough to ask her about the market bill. Assuring me that she was able to get everything she needed with the leftover money from before. I apologized to her and thanked her for her dedication and hard work. She only smiled and nodded thank you back, keeping on with what she was doing.

The walk to the office was almost a run for Hardwick, as he panted trying to keep pace with me.

We rounded the corner right as the young woman that was to be our first appointment hailed a cab. She turned towards us when I called her by name, waving to her while fumbling the keys into the lock. Put off, but still a lady, she walked back to the office as Hardwick held the door open for her. My apology had been accepted once more today. This time because she was a regular patient, and I had never been late before.

We finished the day without any other problems and played as much as talked on the walk home.

11 April, 1888

Men and women gasped at the sight of blood seeping into their clothes. The sharp steel in his hand had made several deep cuts as he moved through my dreams. Warmth being given to the blade from each victim—till it appeared as a branding iron with rivulets of crimson running down each side of the edge. The ones involved feeling no more than a brushing, as someone moved past them in the crowd. The vision encouraged me to my tonic—a few draws later let me rest again as I collapsed across the bed.

Daybreak had shifted the light in the room. Darkness fled under the baseboards, concealing itself behind the walls. Wind pulled heavy on the shutters as they rattled trying to break free of their restraints. The constant noise wormed it's way into my brain giving no choice except retreat.

Margaret was busy with cooking dinner but had a few morsels I could eat before leaving the house.

Retrieving the walking stick from my study it was time for a brisk walk into the city. It had been cleaned after the last walk, but still the blade latch under the knob needed to be checked. With a click the blade slid out smoothly as the stick fell away into my hand. Snapping it back together and positioning a top hat, we headed down the front stairs to the street. Turning west, I proceeded to the Chapel. Feeling rain in the air made me wish I had worn a different coat, but I was not returning home. It was late as it was, and I would do good in making it there before dark. Anyway, rain and darkness brings out the best of the worst. Those are whom I search for in this cover. Like looking for roebuck in the woods you must scout in order to find the trophy. Likewise I would have to scout to find the trophy we desired.

I went back to where I had company of the mongrel, and to see if tonight there may be another show of passion to watch, and perhaps participate. Soon a scheme was developing in the alleyway — as a half dozen Molls led their Fat Culls in by the arm ready too pinch every pound from them. The debauchery proved delightful, as the men wandered out lighter in the purse, and satisfied with their investment. Scouting would have to continue elsewhere. None were the trophy that I sought.

12 April, 1888

Frederick came by the office this morning, as the teapot sounded, talking about how a lunatic had run through a crowd. Cutting more than a bakers dozen as he passed through. Frederick had no clues as to who it was. The people cut didn't even know when it happened till they saw blood. His only thought was it had to have been a razor, for as smooth and quick the blade entered each victim. I had no intent to tell him of my visions, and his case was valid, so correcting him seemed futile at the time. Offering him a cup he shook his head and pointed to the desk drawer. He wanted something a bit stronger to help him through this day. Retrieving the bottle and a couple of cigars brought the lids of his eyes together while he talked his way through the case. He seemed more relaxed upon leaving. Thanking me for the company, and listening to his story, as he bid his leave.

Hardwick ran in the office around one o'clock with an urgent message from his Lordship. The old curmudgeon was accusing me of taking advantage of his niece's innocence and wanted me back at his house that night. Comparing the note to the one in my desk showed that the writing was different but somehow the same. Was this another game of Brite's or really from him? The money earned from our endeavors was too much to ignore his demands. Going back to the house in a hurry with the boy, I prepared myself for the journey, thinking of what I would need as Howard turned the corner in the carriage already packed for the trip. Pulling the horses up, he leapt to the ground and steadied them as I took over the driver's seat. Leaving him with Hardwick to finish the walk home.

Pulling between the gates made my stomach turn as the manor loomed before the carriage. A sudden realization of the voice of the Keeper jumped to the front of my brain. It was his. The carriage turned slightly as the horses stopped for the fresh grasses on the side of the drive; my hands no longer held the reigns before me. My mind raged against me trying to make sense of these delicate situations.

What was this game that he was now playing with me? Does Brite even know who her uncle is? The feared Keeper of the East End only allowed those of the order to ever see him. Why would she know the police do not even know who he is? Why would a child like her know more than the Metropolitan Police?

Where does the man with the knife work into this game? How is he connected to me, or to the Keeper?

Wanting to turn and flee, I convinced myself that someone would have seen me by now and be coming out to check if anything was wrong. The rigging rattled as the horses were edged forward with trembling hands. There was no movement about the estate as the gap closed to the manor. A single shot breached the air, shattering wood above my left shoulder. The horses, used to the noise of the city, didn't even twitch an ear. Plodding steadily, straight ahead, and never minding the person that stepped out from behind a statue holding a rifle on us. The frail form was undeniable as another shot rang out as wood above my right shoulder flew. Brite jumped up and down laughing when I ducked from the wood. Waving as she set the rifle down, running and jumping up on the side of the carriage before I could even stop the horses, she wrapped her arms around my neck kissing me brazenly. It was another game to her.

His Lordship was not here, and she knew that I would come if I thought that he had summoned me.

Tonight was lively as I submitted to Brite's wanton desires.

13 April, 1888

Brite was awake before the sun, laying bare on the chaise oiling her rifle. It laid between her thighs as she ran the cloth up and down the barrel bringing out the muted colors in the metal and woodgrain. Picking up the candle she dripped some of the wax onto the wood stock splattering some on herself as well. Looking me over she pushed against the butt firmly as her hands continued to smooth the wax on the stock. Biting her lip a little harder with each drop that splashed onto her. Finally a drop of blood trickled from the corner of her mouth as the chaise shaked violently with her motions. Her breathing relaxed as she came to me in bed, moist with desire, kissing me profoundly. The taste of blood still on her lips increased my lust, as I fed upon her once again. Crashing through new territories and exploring forbidden boundaries, we awoke the sun from its slumber. Bathing each other before going downstairs to walk the gardens. She made me feel like a young school boy again, as we caressed each other in the tub. His Lordship would shoot me dead without a doubt if he knew of my actions with his ward. Although, when I'm with her death is far from my mind.

The day was wonderful a gray mist still present on the English country-side, and the gardens laid out magnificently by the master gardener. Strolling between the flowers with Brite, the scent of her perfume mixing with the aroma of the petals gave one a heady sensation, as thoughts went back to her bedroom. What once was a fantasy was now so much more.

Returning to the main house the carriage had been repaired with no sign of damage to the wood where Brite had placed two well aimed bullets. The horses had been washed, brushed, and all the harnesses had been polished by the stable hand ready for the trip home. Two baskets set in the back, one of fresh herbs I had not gathered before, and another of food and wine, along with my laundered clothes folded and tied with a ribbon. The servants in their cryptic ways were telling me it was time for me to leave, giving me an excuse if I was to meet his Lordship on the road home. Kissing Brite one more time she slipped a token in my pocket. I whispered to her my love as the road beckoned on before me.

My mind wondered at how such secrets could be kept within such a place, and how many more would be kept there.

14 April, 1888

Returning home last night I had not come across his Lordship but questions abound from Hardwick about what the urgent matter was. Assuring him that it was just about some special herbs, I pulled out the basket telling him to get the book on herbs and identify each bundle to tag them. His face lit up, grabbing the basket, and headed to the house, almost falling as he bound up the stairs to the kitchen. Savant had a look of suspect to my answer. She could read me better than anyone ever in my life. She noticed every expression, eye movement, stance, and movement no matter how small. Not a bad talent except she knew when I was lying — and she knew that what I told Hardwick was not the whole of the matter.

Savant had not come to my bed last night. When I woke she was sitting in the chair across the room, fully clothed, watching me. I had never been known to talk in my sleep, but the look on her face told me she knew more than what I had told Hardwick. Getting out of the chair, she left the room without a word. What did she know? The token on the table told me enough, a rose scented handkerchief with a young girls initials, laid smooth on the marble. My coat hung over the back of the chair, brushed free of the dust from the ride home and a large red A stitched across its back. Since the night at the theatre she had been my constant companion. I would have to come up with a reason for having it if I wished for it to continue.

Dark clouds also dominated the sky, keeping the sun from bathing the house with its light— causing a gloom in my study that almost matched my own. The issue of Savant weighed heavy on me. Talking to her would be the way to diminish the pain in her, or allow myself to be able to get some work done. I sent Hardwick to the basement to bundle and hang the herbs and send Savant to my office. Savant came with a scowl of discontent which burnt through me. I moved to close and lock the door. Tears streamed down her face as she started on me with questions and fist. Before I thought a sharp backhand sent her to the floor. Quickly moving to her side as blood came from the split in her lip all she said was "Why?" Trying to explain that his Lordship's niece had a schoolgirls crush on me and had given the token to me before I left the manor seemed to have little affect. Only after taking her into my arms and gently pressing my lips to hers did she seem to calm. The taste of her blood in that kiss ignited my heart to her. As the rest of the household gathered on the landing, I decided not go out this night.

The sound of footsteps moving in all directions was heard as I placed the key in the door to unlock it. Savant just smiled and shook her head as she took my hand and led me back to the bedroom.

15 April, 1888

reams invaded me. The man with the knife stood over a body stretched out on a table. A lateral cut made down the torso, blood flowed down a channel in the table, to a hole, and collected in a bucket underneath. Hands reached and pulled the skin back, revealing the organs, before scooping the intestines out to study what laid beneath. A quick cut separated them from the stomach, dumping its contents into the cavity. Stench permeated the room, as bile was unshackled to explore the creases and folds inside the bowl that held it. A tube punctured through the side of the body letting the bile flow freely with the blood. He searched the cavity, prodding the remaining items in detail with the knife, removing them one by one. Like he was disassembling a machine he placed each in order of removal along the side of the table. A smile of acknowledgment gave me the look of a madman, as he removed everything down to the spine. Everything had been removed cleanly except for the bowels. He seemed satisfied with his work, before throwing it all into a furnace.

Savant rolled over, kissing me good morning, as if the fight between us had never happened. Removing myself from her grasp and pouring a small portion of the hot water from the tea kettle into the shaving mug, I whipped up a rich lather with the brush. Savant still naked, picked up the razor, checked the edge, gave it a few swipes on the strap, and kissing the blade before sitting me down in the chair, to lather my face. When it came to using her wiles was there anything she could not do for a man? Most would call me crazy for letting a woman that I had fought with the day before shave me, but trust has to develop somehow. She finished by pouring some water from the pitcher over the cloth in the basin and freshening my body with the cool water. Helping me with my clothes she finally put on a lace top. Which did not help me to concentrate on the rest of the day. Her nipples protruding through the fabric, and her bottom half still remaining uncovered, made me wander into other non-productive thoughts. Thoughts better left till I get home again.

Breakfast was prepared when I entered the dining room, a cup of hot tea waiting at my place, and steaming fresh bread on the table. Margaret emerged from the kitchen with a platter of fried cutlets ladened with scallions and white wine gravy.

I did find the meal hardy and delightful as always when Margaret cooked, but as normal work won out over a second helping. Gathering my things, I took directly to town, as several crows found flight when the front door closed.

Walking allows me time to think, process, develop plans, and to daydream. This morn I needed to do all of the first items, yet alone I could only do the last. Daydreaming of Savant, Brite, and of Hardwick one day taking over the business. Of course the man with the knife interrupted each one with my own psychotic voice. He keeps pressing me to follow him. He's the one that first led me to the Shadows. He's also the one that helps keep me safe in the Chapel, so why would I not follow him?

Today was a day of pondering. No one came in the office: no patients, not Frederick, not even Hardwick to distract me. At three thirty I locked the door and headed to the club to meet up, as some of the boys would sure to be there by the time I arrived. It wasn't that it was a long walk, but I could take my time wandering through the East Side and maybe find a trinket for Savant.

Men I partially recognized but didn't know spoke to me by name as I walked the East Side. Could they be part of the Shadows, or just knew me from my practice? Either way I had been noticed and confirmed. Strolling from booth to booth, the tapping of my cane against the stones, lulling me into a trance, a small hand grasped mine. Turning, the girl with the doll walked quietly beside me, holding my hand. Her smile so infectious, I missed the distraction, as a boy lifted my purse, till a scruffy booth attendant handed it back to me with a wary look. Looking from him and back to her I told her to go on and play elsewhere. I thanked the man and handed him a copper before continuing on my way. Greeting me in brotherly fashion he suggested "something for a lady friend?" holding out a fine necklace. Quality of which not expected to be seen in the East Side. I asked him how much. "To you, sir, no charge, maybe it will help you get back into her good grace" was all he said. He placed it into a small cloth bag and handed it to me, bidding a good day. No one gave anything for nothing in the East Side, so why did he give me a necklace that he could easy get five pounds for? How did he know about my fight with Savant, or that I had been in a fight with anyone? I went home without going to the club.

16 April, 1888

Savant showed me how much she appreciated the necklace I presented her with last night. Breakfast in bed and a special tea that she had made with the herbs and flowers I had come in with. While eating she warmed pachouli oil to rub on my feet and calves, as the bath was being drawn. Her hands pulling tension out through the soles of my feet. Parts of my body relaxed that I didn't even know was hurting till that moment. The bath was luxurious, taking away the rest of my fears and doubts about our relationship. I do not know what god sent her to me, but at this time I am thankful.

The weather was miserable for going into the Chapel, but need of talking to His Lordship was imperative. The cold rain and snow made bones anguish for warmth, as the drudgery of walking terminated feeling in my feet. His Lordship greeted me with a hug and kisses which I have tried to get accustomed to.

Showing a bottle of Cognac to him and pointing to some chairs I asked "how did you become the Keeper?"

His lordship explained. "My father had owned most of the buildings in the Chapel back when it thrived. When he was killed in a factory, which is the home of the Shadows now, I took over. It was better times and people came to depend on my kindness and strength. Time went on and I started the organization to help protect the good people here and punish those that might mean them harm. You are the first one that I have let into our group that is not from here. Why did you want to join?"

I didn't expect the question and didn't know how to answer. I did not tell him of what exactly I sought— except for a cure to help restore Elizabeth. My connection to him as one of the Shadows allowed me to talk freely, but I still gauged my words carefully. Any mention of the man with the knife shall have questions of intent. Till I know why he kept coming to me, or the visions of his deeds, I could not divulge any knowledge of him. I did ask him one more question, "Does Brite know that you are the Keeper?"

He bellowed with laughter. "No, that child has no knowledge of my business or the ways of the world."

Apparently he had no idea of what she was capable of knowing. Including her seduction of me.

We both chuckled now, as the Cognac began to take its toll on us.

Bidding him farewell, after some more talk of business, he arranged for a carriage to take me home. This ride was much better than the last one, being able to sit in a seat instead of the floor, and without a gunny sack over my head. The driver knew exactly where to go, dropping me off at the house. I handed the driver a coin for his trouble.

17 April, 1888

Meeting with his Lordship last night put some fears aside as it raised others. Could I trust his household or Brite? The secrets about me at his home with her, when he was not there, could ruin our business together. Even though he has tried to trap me with a house maid in my bed, that was not his charge. He could kill me, and no one would question it once he told his story of the event.

I cannot worry about what could be at this time. He was clueless about what was happening in his own home. Much less what I had been doing or my protector, the man with the knife. Anyways, the Shadows would have told him, if there was anything to report that concerned him or the organization. They seemed to be keeping up with my house and office more than anything else I might do. My care would need to be what happens in the Chapel, and in my business with him.

Snow laid in deep swirls as trees hung heavy with the weight. Only the most desperate would be out today. Any movement out could be tracked. Not wanting our movements to be known, finishing my documentation would be the order of today. Besides, there was always Savant to distract me. Should I need her.

18 April, 1888

The snow had turned to a gray and brown slush from wagons delivering goods. Stepping into the office helped little from the cold, being able to see each breath Hardwick and I took. I sent him straight down to fire the boiler. The steam would soon heat the place up for customers.

Today was the day Hardwick had been waiting for. Narcissa wanted a complete physical and had asked me to do it for her. He had been asking every day if she was coming. This morning he had not said anything about it.

"Hardwick, get the exam room ready for Narcissa's exam."

"Sir, yes sir, right on it sir."

"Do you know what all I need?"

"I think so, sir."

"Let me know as soon as you are done, so I can check it."

"I will sir, thank you sir."

"What are you thanking me for?"

Hardwick blushed from head to toe. "Oh um, I don't know sir, but thank you."

"Well okay, but you need to hurry. Howard will have her here shortly in the carriage."

He ran from the room like it was on fire. I sat there thinking what must be going through the boy's head. Metal clanged and glass rattled down the hall, before I heard boots slapping the floor back to my office.

"It's done sir."

"Okay, I will be there in just a minute."

Hardwick stood at the door, looking at me, till I got up and went with him to the room. There were a few things out of place, and we got them put in order as the front bell jingled. Hardwick jumped at the sound then composed himself as he walked down the hall to greet his teacher. Leading her down the hall to the room where I waited, but frowning deeply as I excused him from the room and closed the door. After the exam, and her leaving, I found Hardwick sitting at my desk still sulking.

"Why didn't you let me stay? You have let me stay for others?"

"It wouldn't of been right. She is you teacher, and the others are just patients to you. You would not be able to learn properly from her if I had let you stay. You would have never been able to look at her the same, now would you?"

"But—"

"You know what I'm talking about, now don't you."

"Yes sir."

"Now go and set the room again for our next patient."

Slowly without a word he walked down the hall, barely talking to me the rest of the day, feeling that I had betrayed him.

19 April, 1888

Well the little bastard was still visibly upset with me, turning away, as I spoke to him. Grabbing him by his coat I pulled him out of his chair, dragging him into the parlor, throwing him onto the couch backwards.

"Now stay there Hardwick, we need to talk."

"I have nothing to say to you."

"Well good, then sit there and listen. I brought you into my house, family, and business. You are not going to disrespect me this way. Unless you want me to deposit you back the way I found you."

"But you treat me like a child. I'm not a child."

"I thought you had nothing to say to me?"

Hardwick tried to get up on that statement, thinking he was going to walk away from me. I pushed him back to the couch. "Then prove it with your actions. You will do as I command or else. Can I trust you to be my proxy or not?"

"Yes sir, you can. You have treated me with nothing but kindness, sir—I should be ashamed of my actions. Will you teach me how to control myself as you do, only showing my anger when proper?"

"I have told you before to watch and listen more than speaking. If you have a question, ask. There is much you need to learn. I will do as much as I can to teach you, but if you treat me in an off manner I can find a place for you elsewhere. Replacing you with another would be no trouble. Have I made myself understood to you? It will depend on you, but as far as I'm concerned we need never speak of this subject again. Have I assumed correctly?"

"You have, sir. I will make you proud of your choice in me. I'm terribly sorry, sir."

"Excellent, now let's get our breakfast. We have much to do today."

The last part was not totally the truth. I had much for him to do, now that he understood his ensnarement to me.

Arriving to the office early I set Hardwick on cleaning every bottle and instrument in the place with orders for him to scrub the walls and floors when he was done. Sitting down at the desk the front bell rang on the door. Hardwick announced that a bloody blue bottle was out front. Something about another cutting and Frederick.

"Send him back."

"Sorry to bother you sir, but the inspector would like for you to come down to the precinct."

"No problem, my good man. What seems to be the matter with our good inspector this morning? Not another body is it?"

"Well sir, it seems so. Pulled from the river at daybreak. Another union organizer from what we can tell."

"Humph another organizer—Hardwick, I will be back as soon as I can. Till then you are in charge."

"Yes sir. What should I tell people if they ask where you are at."

"I'm out on business. That is all they need to know."

"Right sir, out on business sir, got it."

What the blue bottle did not tell me was the method of death, or who had been found. A woman, around mid twenties, with a single cut to the neck that scraped the spinal column. Beat beyond recognition before being killed and deposited in the river. The union pin on her lapel the only means of identity. Inspection of her further indicated that she had been mercilessly raped and sodomized, either during or before the beating. This wasn't going to be easy on Frederick.

"Good morning ole chap."

"What's so damned good about it? Have you not seen that poor girl in there? Do you think she is having a good morning?"

"I've seen her. Looks like someone is trying to send one hell of a message. Do you know who she might be yet?"

"Nothing. No one has reported her missing, and we don't even know if the pin she was wearing is hers or was pinned on her."

"Frederick, I can tell you this. Whoever killed her took their time. It's not the same person that has done the other attacks."

"How do you know that?"

"It was almost definitely more than one person, and they took extreme privilege with her before they killed her. They fucked her repeatedly, ripping her arse hole and vagina till they bleed her. I found seaman in both cavities. It would be hard for one man to do so much damage like that."

"So we are looking for some really sick fuckers on this one?"

"I'm afraid so, and probably a group of them hired by someone to do this type of work."

"Thank you for the help."

Reaching into my coat, and withdrawing a larger bottle of tonic. "Here, maybe this will make it a better morning."

He got a glass and poured the tonic like a whiskey. Knocking it back, he poured another before trying to hand it back.

"Keep it. I have another."

A calmness washed over him as the door shut.

Frederick had every right for his concerns. The men he had now would never be able to solve all the cases they had, and that is only in his precinct. I cannot fathom why anyone would want the job even if he was able to hire more. The money is atrocious, hours even worse, family life non-existent. Damn ignorant bastards.

I looked through the glass of my office front door. Hardwick was working on, or shall I say playing with, the two plate mirrors that covered the opposite walls in the waiting room. He straightened up, and looked around for his rag that was hanging out of his back pocket when he heard the bell clatter above the door.

"How is your work coming?"

"Sir, I was just finishing up in here."

"Yes, I saw how you were finishing up. They are fascinating are they not?"

"I've never seen myself like that before."

"Most people have not. I use them to reflect on all the different aspects of my life."

He had that distant look in his eyes as he gazed deeper into the reflections.

"Now back to work, and be sure to polish all the brass, too. We can play later."

"Yes — sir."

It was late afternoon when Hardwick came to the office reporting he had finished.

"Are you positive that you got everything?"

"I, um, I believe so, sir."

"Well then, let's have a look. Show me what all you have done."

There were a few items he could have done better, but overall he had done considerable and needed rewarding. The pastry shop down the block would do. He stared at the window every time we passed it.

"Come with me my young man, let's go on an excursion."

"Where to, sir?"

"Does it matter as long as we enjoy it? Anyway you have worked hard all day, and it's long past closing hours. There will be time for more work tomorrow. Now get your coat boy, or I'll lock the door and you can stay here till I return."

"Coming sir."

"You're not yet, but that will change before the night's over."

Being only about thirteen, or a few more, he did not understand the reference; although, that would soon be a past memory to him.

The bakery was a short ways from our door, and as always Hardwick had run ahead of me, not noticing the turn into the shop. I stood inside the shop, waiting to see how long it would be before he found me. His eyes popped wide open in disbelief of where I was standing. With a slight motion of the hand, he almost broke the door trying to enter.

"Boy, pick what you want. It's my treat to you for a hard days work."

"Really sir, anything?"

"Within reason, now quit wasting time, we have other places to go before journeying homeward."

He wrangled me to purchase more than I had expected before we left the shop carrying a bag of scented wonders. Anyway, they would be good bait for the lasses tonight.

20 April, 1888

Hardwick started as the young little bastard that I had found on the street after replacing his former owner a few weeks ago. Now he is an intricate section of my life, that needs to train more for his life than mine. Last night was a small taste of how people could be manipulated with the smallest trinkets. The diffident child became brash as the night went on. Coyly enticing the girls to him and his sweets. By the end of our outing none of them were safe from the dreadful creature I had brought forth.

21 April, 1888

estraint in desire is not a large commodity in our house. Hardwick was coming into his own on this account. Not showing any attempt in curbing this fact on his own, I will need to intercede. He is too licentious from his previous life to be turned loose. I will have to watch him close, as he has a tendency for cruelty. He has been witnessed devouring small animals. Sometimes while they still live. Crunching them between sharp points of teeth. Not once thinking about how those actions would appear to others. Fear is practically void in him, as darkness grows inside. The night I took him out, he performed unspeakable acts with a girl younger than himself. She was the daughter of the whore servicing me and had never been with a man; although she had watched her whore mother take care of men most of her young life. His old master had called him Crowley "wood of crows". I fear one day that he will return back to that, only more educated thanks to his new benefactor. He absolutely struts around, as a crow would, with his blackness showing for all to see. He has already showed interest to train in different gnostic and spiritual arts. His questions are becoming deeper, more difficult, and increasingly confusing for me to answer. I'm an educated man that can hold my own in any conversation, but with Hardwick's questions and reasoning, I feel more like the student than the teacher. Of all the children in London, why was this beast dropped into my life?

22 April, 1888

The bell from the front door clanged across the floor as glass shattered against the wall. Boots came clomping down the hall. A muddled Blue Bottle carrying a young bruised and bleeding girl yelled for help.

"What happened to her?"

"I don't know. She was found outside the workhouse this morning. Can you help her?"

"She has been beaten bad. It does not appear that who ever did this wanted her to live. Unless they did want her to live."

"What do you mean doc?"

"There has been no hard blows to any area of her fragile body that would cause death. It seems to have been more of a warning to her or someone. You say that she was found outside the workhouse. A place that people would surely notice her soon enough to get help."

"That makes no sense. Why would they beat this poor girl?"

"She or someone close to her may have seen, or know something that they shouldn't. Before you ask. She is a whore off the street, it could be anything, there is no way of telling unless she tells you. I doubt that will happen."

"Why would she not tell me?"

"First of all, your a Copper, Blue Bottle, worst of the

worst to a child off the street. She has been told her whole
life not to trust any of you. You want her to confide in
you now. You may have had a chance if you had caught
the person that beat her before hand, and protected her
from them, but you weren't there now were you?"

"I guess not."

"Hell, boy you know you weren't, or she would not
be in this condition now, would she? Get your damn
head out of your arse, and look at this child. This is what
you are hired to protect. Now get the hell out of my
office, and do your job. I will take care of her for now."

"You shall not talk to me like that."

"I will talk to you any damn way I please. If you do
not like it we can go down and talk to Frederick about
it. Would that be more suited to you? No? Then get your
arse back out on that street, and do your damn job."

The Blue Bottle looked at me with hatred, but he
knew that I was right as he excused himself from the
room. Given time he will make a good officer. Hopefully
he wont get himself killed before then.

Now what shall I do with this child, the same one
that Hardwick had fucked so forcibly only days ago?
I did not know why, but could feel his hand in her
condition now. Had he done this for his own pleasure,
because he could, or to protect me in some way? He has
been studying all of the medical books in the office. Does
he have enough knowledge already, or am I accusing
him too quickly? The only way to know would be talk to
him about it, and determine if he has anything to hide.

23 April, 1888

After staying with the girl all night she would recover from her injuries physically, but not her mental state. Her mother had started her on her course with Hardwick. Since then others had been introduced to her, and last night in her drugged state I had pleasured myself with her. The only thing to do with her now is to commit her to the asylum. Where whatever babbling she would utter would be dismissed as that of a lunatic. Being a doctor myself they would not question it, and thus protecting Hardwick in the process.

Midday I hired an errand boy to fetch an ambulance to carry the girl to the County Asylum.

24 April, 1888

Savant had spoken out of her place to Narcissa about the girl. Hardwick, ears keener than most dogs, listened from the other room hearing their whole conversation. Till I get home to punish her properly she is chained and locked in the cellar. The rest will leave her be, and to me. I think I shall bring home a few friends to introduce her to. Then she shall show them geniality whether she is up to it or not.

Soon as he found out what I had done, Hardwick wanted to go get the girl and bring her home as his pet. I would have none of it.

There is death behind his eyes. That alone makes him dangerous to all around him. As the moth lives in the same neighborhood as the spider. It knows that they could never live in the same house. This is how it would be with Hardwick and the girl. While they might be able to exist in the same city, she would soon become an avaricious source of amusement for his twisted mind. One reason he was made my neophyte is how his mind works. He sleeps little yet can still concentrate on massive amounts of knowledge presented to him. Under proper care he will one day surpass all of my accomplishments. Turning my name into nothing that would be remembered. Except, perhaps, when I heal Elizabeth in her sleeping ailment. When we find her cure we will be as famous as Mary made Victor. People

155

will write about me for decades, maybe centuries. First we must locate the proper parts for her cure, fresh clean parts. Victor is not the only one that can solve the great mysteries. We can also. No matter how long the search.

His Lordship, the Keeper of East Side, and the Chapel must be consulted. His au fait of plant-pathology shall be of tremendous guidance to my hands. Grapes injected with the right tincture could assist in propagandizing a young lady that might otherwise, let us say, object to the nights activities.

25 April, 1888

The message sent to his lordship had been conceded. He had in turn — requested I meet him at the estate two days hence. His Lordship is latitudinally fair with most dealings as long as they profit him. The questions, howeve, would need to be prepared to reduce any questionable discernment. I would at least have time before the meeting with the old bastard.

I had the library alone. The club was quiet for a change, most of the daily patrons were attending the funeral of a prominent member. There were more important things on mind than listening to someone praise some horse's arse that never gave you the time of day when alive. There is no way to endear a man with his qualities. If they told the truth about him, they would need to burn him for his next travels. Least I'm not being bothered listening to how great he was and how he will be missed. Now I sit here in solitude working, drinking, and hurting for my father.

26 April, 1888

He is dead; that is all that needs to be known. How else am I suppose to react to the man that disowned me before I was born and had my mother locked up just because he got a whore pregnant. Yes he made sure I was taken care of, and got schooling, but he never acknowledged me. Even when I became a member of the club he showed me nothing but disdain. I surely was not going to show him more now.

Savant lays beside me each night, my constant bed companion will never have those worries placed on her. I know that she loves me as much as a young girl can that is given a better way of life. She would do anything to protect me, to care for me, and to live for me by my side.

27 April, 1888

The questions are formulated. The Carriage is packed, cleaned, and hitched. Fog from the Moor has coated the city. Savant spent all night making sure she would not be forgotten while begging me to take her with me.

"But why? I will make the drive one most pleasurable to you."

"Savant— I told you that I need to talk business. You would be a distraction to me if you were there."

"You never take me with you. Are you ashamed to be with me?"

"I am a guest at his Lordship's manor. It would not be right to show up with you. He asked for me, to come and talk. He did not ask for me to bring you or any one else with me."

"But—"

"I said no. Now get it through your childish head."

"I only wanted—"

"I don't care what you wanted; you are not going."

The bitch would really know how little I care if she found out about Brite. The drive would be a miserable one, and her offer any other time, but I will be with Brite tonight. Neither girl would want to share me with the other. But I can fantasize about it. One an expert in the art of sex; the other so beautiful just the thought of being with her engorges a man.

Driving in the fog is miserable, and even in this gloom people care not about themselves. The reins on the horses have to be held tight, as people walk about still drunk from the night before, or lack of food and a good place to rest. An old whore steps under the horses not paying heed to her life or the loss of it. Should I run her down? If it would not put me behind on my travels; I would have instead of pulling them up. I care little of these maggots, their existence little more than eating the rotten flesh of this city. Why should I? They come to me for help, but never have money to pay for my service. The nuisance of my days on this earth. How else shall I treat them, the vermin they are? Soon I shall be out of this city, retreating to my own thoughts, and daydream of the possibilities that could be.

Outside the city gates a man laid in the road, blood matted in his hair. Instinct had taught me to pull my pistol out, as I came to a stop several meters from where he lay. This time instinct was correct; the man jumped to his feet while two others emerged from the brush, firearms in hand. Getting a clean shot into the shoulder of the one to my right reaching for the reins. Spiriting the horses forward I ran down the one that had been laying in the road. Startled by the reaction the one to the left fumbled with his rifle dropping it in the mud as the carriage wheel struck him in the side. These rats had come out of the city, predators looking to kill and feed. Today they became the prey of one that kills with jocularity, uncaring about their well being, concerned only for himself.

Reaching the house, Brite met me at the door. His Lordship had left all my questions to her, as he was called away on business. This convenience was an almost predictable outcome to me, being at the manor. After the first meeting; she had managed for him to be gone each time since.

Finding out that she is the master herbalist was a pleasant surprise. Except for the knowledge that she is the one that drugged me the first night I stayed at the manor.

"So sir, how is Savant? That is what you call her, is it not?"

"What, how do you know about Savant?"

"Have you not wondered where she learned all of her skills, or who sent her to you? She could have answered all your questions, but then you wouldn't be here with me."

"So you are the one that taught her about plants?"

"Among...other things. She is my eyes and ears in your house and the city."

"But I did not even know you, or your uncle, when she came to me."

"That does not mean that we did not know of you, though."

"Then does that mean that she..."

"Yes she knows all about us, and has played her part. Had you brought her like she asked, you would have had a night beyond the fantasy that made you smile the way here."

"Why did she not tell me?"

"As in your household it was not her place, and she is paid well to keep my secrets. Like all the staff is here."

"Where does your uncle work into this?"

"First of all, he is not my uncle as you were led to believe. After I inherited all that you see, I needed someone to take care of my affairs that would not be challenged. I found him in a prison, waiting to be sent to the gallows. In return for me saving him from his fate he agreed to play the head of this household and become the Keeper of the east side."

"That makes you the head of the Shadows."

"They do my bidding so to speak, through him. He never does anything without my permission first. Have you not thought it strange? That it takes him at least a day or two to grant your request. Under the oath you took; I'm trusting you not to let this information ever leave your lips. You understand the penalty should you fail to do so."

"I know the oath, and that it works both ways."

"Then we have an agreement you will keep my secrets and sell the herbs in London. In return, I and Savant will do whatever you want from us."

"Shall we start now then my lovely?"

Unbuttoning her top— "anything you desire."

"Send a carriage for Savant then."

"My dear sir, anything you desire shall be done.."

Her dress descended to the floor as she crossed the room, stepping out of it with such grace of practice. A hand grazed across my trousers bringing out my lust. How many men has she devoured, this Succubus. Luring them in with her innocents. Making them think they were her first, by planning it with her cycle. So clever, so devious, I think I love her more now.

Before I could cleave the thought of her bare arse leaving the room, she was coming back in. A nude handmaiden of tolerable beauty followed close behind. Collars around her neck, wrist, and ankles were combined with small chains making a jangle as she walked. Brite, holding the other end of the chains, turned offering a cigar and brandy from the silver tray the girl held.

"Let us celebrate our understanding while we wait on Savant to arrive. She should be here in less than an hour. Anyway, I want to see what you have in store for us tonight before she gets here. "

"But Brite, I just now told you to send for her. How could she possibly be here that soon?"

"I knew that you would not bring her with you in fear that it would ruin something between us. I told her to start on her way here an hour or so after you left the house."

"What if I had not wanted any one else except you tonight?"

"Then you would have never known that she had been here. You and I both know that would never have been an issue. You daydreamed the whole way here about being in bed with us both. Now did you not? Are we going to talk all night, or are you going to fuck the slave I have here for you."

The girl laid down on the tabletop in the middle of the room, while Brite pulled the chains tight, and fastened them underneath. Opening a drawer on the table side she pulled a riding crop out, and placed it in my hand, before bending over to kiss the girls breast. The girl's nipples became erect as so did I. Brite looked over her shoulder at me then down to the whip, let me know what she wanted next. A soft moan escaped her lips as the flat of the crop struck her bare skin. With each strike her moans became louder. Abruptly she turned her attention to me, grabbing my manhood and pulling it toward the girl's awaiting holes, as her other hand caressed her own. She climbed onto the table to straddle the girls face. She lowered herself down on the girl as I penetrated her. The girl let out a slight whimper, as I forced myself into her. Hearing a thumping sound behind me in the corner, I looked to find Savant reclining on the chaise feverishly pleasuring herself as she watched us. How long she had been there I did not know, but the cushion was wet from her eager work. After seeing me watch her for a moment she casually stood, and walked over to me, taking the whip from my hand. A quick flip of her wrist brought the leather down wickedly ripping my flesh. The pleasure of pain causing me to explode inside the girl. Brite pushed me out of the girl and greedily took the whole of my manhood into her mouth, her tongue swirling around the head and shaft of it, making me discharge harder than before. Causing my legs to shake, as to not hold my weight. Savant steadied me from behind as Brite lapped at the girl's neither region, drawing out every drop of me. When she was done she climbed off the table, leaving the girl chained where she was. Savant lead me to the chaise and lowered herself on top of me as she reached for Brite's taught body. Sucking one of her pink nipples into her mouth and smartly biting the tip till a trickle of red showed on her white teeth. Brite jerked Savant's head back by the hair, kissing her then down to kiss me. The taste of iron and lust still on her lips.

28 April, 1888

Last night was stupendous. Although I still have no idea who or when they unchained the girl from the table. When Brite led Savant and I to the garden she was still there. Passed out from what ever drug Brite had concocted for her.

We played in the labyrinth and fountains acting out parts of Shakespears' Midsummer Night. Finally reaching the center where a table was prepared with fruits, cheeses, and wines from around the world. The girls, still in their frisky mood laid me down on a bench feeding my belly as well as my eyes. Having their way with each other for my enjoyment as well as their own.

This morning I woke in bed with the two of them, how I got there was blurry, except that it was not on my own. Brite had somehow done it to me again. The only difference was this time I allowed her to.

All the wine that we drank last night was pleading to escape from me, but the pot was on the other side of the room, and here I lay between two naked sleeping girls. Trying to get out of bed without waking them was to no avail, as they sat up in bed watching me standing naked pissing. My confidence fell as they came to both sides of me to get a better look. Small delicate fingers caressed the burning flesh that was now my body. Red from invasion, and closeness of their breath caused a chill up my spine. What plans these two had in store was of little concern. What else could happen after all the debauchery from last night? Finishing my business they both took turns, as if it was natural for them to relive themselves in front of others. Finishing they both pulled me backwards throwing themselves on top of me in the downy mattress. The night games were to continue.

29 April, 1888

Brite gave me the herbs and knowledge that I needed. Showing me how to inject grapes with a small needle at the base of each stem. Assuring that the tincture would not kill used this way, but the more someone ate, the less in control they would become. After some practice it was undetectable which ones had been injected. The true Keeper had given me permission, and her trust.

I have been given illumination these few days. Savant would administer the grapes to Narcissa, eating them with her, although from a different part of the platter. She had wanted to taste the stuffy whore from the day she became Hardwick's teacher. Hardwick would just find a bowl in his room with a note from me thanking him for watching the shop while I was away. In this way I could learn even more about the time, and amount consumed, prior to obtaining what I wanted from a young lady.

Visions of the man with the knife constantly invade my mind. He saw me with Brite, the whore chained to the table, and Savant in our lust. His eyes glowed red as he bent over her, tasting the blood oozing from the marks left by the whip while ramming harder with each thrust. He saw us in the garden, and the bedroom. I could not see him in the garden, but I could sense his every movement. Would he also see the plans I had devised for Savant, Narcissa, and Hardwick?

Savant's dry humor had Narcissa almost laughing while entering the parlor arm in arm. Savant held the key to tonight in her free hand, a platter of cheese with grapes adorning each side. Setting it down on the table with a spin she popped a grape into her mouth from the side facing me. Taking another one from the other side, she fed it to Narcissa, showing me which ones were laced. Narcissa, reclining on the couch feigned being the Queen of Egypt, allowing Savant to feed her from a small bunch of grapes. Lowering it to her mouth so she could pluck each one off with her soft lips. Showing her skill of not breaking the skin. The grape would reappear held suspended by her teeth, before she cut it in half. Pouring myself some brandy the girls asked, "Can we have some?" Why would I say no to these two lovelies? Pouring them both a good snifter without so much as a blink I handed each one. Half way through the glass of brandy Narcissa was showing the effect of the grapes, having eaten about fifteen of them. Her earlier mirth had turned into full giddiness, as Savant lowered the grapes down to her, then pulled them away, before she could get one replacing it with a long kiss. This play would go on for several times before Savant would have Narcissa's top unbuttoned, massaging her ample breast from behind. Narcissa breathed contently as hands traced her outline down to her skirt. Her bosom in full view for me, but under the force of the grapes, she no longer cared that I was in the room, giving in to whatever Savant wanted from her. Motioning for me to come over, Savant fed her a few more, but there was no need. Narcissa was now participating in her own seduction, lifting her skirt to her narrow waist while spreading her legs wide for the next intrusion. Her under garments were soaked and her own hands provided me access to her delicate holes. Tasting the sweet nectar that was flowing liberally now; I scooped some from her pearl. My tongue curled around the sticky droplets, lifting them to Savants waiting lips. Savant, smelling the cream still deposited on my mustache, kissed me greedy for any residue she could find. I Lifted Narcissa to her feet and ripped the skirt and under garments from her body before I took her seat. Positioning her just right, I entered her from behind, her arse tight around my girth. Savant knelt between our legs, her face planted in Narcissa as her fingers played with us both. My organ strained against the firmness it was held in, as my seed dribbled out around it. Savant was there to not let anything go to waste, lapping up anything that might be allowed. She Pulled me out for a thorough cleaning before placing me into Narcissa's tight little cunt. Watching as blood seeped from her, Savant nodded to me that it was done. Flicking Narcissa's taunt nipples made the bitch squirt juices all over Savant's face which made us both smile in satisfaction. Taking the naked whore up to bed was a chore, but worth it. Now I could fuck her the way she needed, and she would wake in the morning between us, sore, but a full woman. How would Narcissa react to this embarrassment? Would she remember what is happening to her, or like me know things up to a point and then nothing? It makes no difference, she will wake up in bed with us in the morning. We will tell her that it was her that suggested it, wanted it, begged for us to be her first. How will she dispute it? She will ask us to never tell anyone of it. Which we will assure her we would never do anything to ruin her reputation, as long as she stayed with us, and of course how could she refuse.

30 April, 1888

Narcissa woke as planned, naked between us, cuddled up with me still inside her. Mortified by what she had done she was ours. She would do whatever we wanted in fear of her being found out. The truth—she enjoyed the feel of a man. A feeling she had never had, and now was afraid she would not get enough of, being shared with another woman. Savant assured her that she had nothing to fear, as she preferred her touch over a man's.

If less than twenty of the grapes would allow us to have our way with a virgin like Narcissa. What would a few more do to a trollop from the street? Tonight we will take the carriage into the Chapel.

The girls were ready as I commanded. Dressed for the night, less undergarments. Savant took the seat in the carriage across from Narcissa and I, a bag of grapes grasped tight, ready for the show that she hoped would commence soon. Offering Narcissa some of the grapes from her bag came with a disapproving look from me. She tucked them away, telling her maybe we should save them for later. "Yes," I said, "you can share them with the lady the two of you fancy tonight.

"Savant, could I trust that when we occur this night that you will send word to my benefactor?"

"Yes, if you wish, sir."

"I think it would be best to keep them in good terms.

Anyway, with the help that they have offered our house I think it is important."

"Do you mind if we stop at the brownstone before we go home, then a friend of mine will meet us there."

"We can do that, but how — oh never mind."

"He will know and be waiting for me."

"Then that will be the last stop before we return."

With a rap on the roof "Howard, drive on".

"Howard is driving?" Narcissa exclaimed.

"Not to worry, my dear, he is more of a confidant than both of you."

The carriage staggered forward as it caught up rhythm with the horse. Jostled inside, my hand slipped between Narcissa's sticks. She jumped from the shock then allowed it to remain. It did not take her long to fall into the fold.

Howard had been given the directions of where I wanted him to take us, but I also took Savant's encouragement as to where we would find the prize we searched for tonight. With the coins in my pocket our endeavor should not take long with the assistance of my two helpers. Savant told me of an area that I had not previously ventured that she thought may be better than the way we were going.

"Give Howard the way, and we will follow you this eve."

"But how will he hear me?"

Grabbing my cane and giving a quick knock on the roof, Howard opened the trap with a "Sir?".

"Now tell him."

"Well, I see, yes, Mr Howard turn left at the next street, our plans have changed some. I will direct you from here on tonight I guess."

"Do as she says my good man."

With a few more turns we were farther into the Chapel than I had ever been. She had taken us to the other side where it backed up to the north side of the city. The crumpets were of better notion than the ones that I had seen in any of my previous excursions.

"How do you know of this area?"

"I worked not far from here sir, before I was apprenticed by lady Brite. She had taken me in and gave me a chance to prove myself of use."

"She is generous that way, is she not?"

"More so than you can imagine sir."

"I'm beginning to see that. Do you two see anything that you like?"

The girls peered out the windows until they both agreed on one. "That one there. She looks very nice." They both pointed to a sweet looking flower standing inside a doorway. Howard pulled up the horse as I opened the door and called to her to come over, pouring a few coins from my purse. Her eyes flashed to the coins as she hastened to the carriage door.

"How can I help you and your ladies govner?" Her eyes never leaving the coins in my hand.

"We would like the pleasure of your company for the night if you are not predisposed."

"It would be my honor sir."

Extending my hand with the coins in it. "Then welcome aboard."

She palmed the coins as she took my hand, and climbed in next to Savant.

"Savant if you please offer our guest some refreshment."

Missing my cue she kissed the girl heavily.

"Savant."

"Yes, I'm sorry would you like something to drink?" She poured some Brandy from the sideboard offering the glass to her.

The girl took it whether she wanted it or not. She knew that she had already accepted payment for this night, and what ever it entailed.

"Now pour some for the rest of us. This is a night for entertainment."

Savant filled three more glasses and passed them around, then looked at me while retrieving the bag. I gave her a nod as she pulled out a bunch of the grapes placing them on the Mahogany fold out.

"Would you like some, Sir?" Savant asked with a devilish grin.

"No, I got those for you ladies to relish. There are plenty more, please help yourselves."

Narcissa looked to the grapes then to the girl. "Oh Dear, I had some of these the other night you must try them."

"What are they?"

"They are the most wonderful juicy orbs in the world," exclaimed Narcissa. "Just pop one in your mouth like this."

The girl looked awkward in her situation having appearance of never being in such refinement before.

Narcissa, taking one from her hand, cut it into with her teeth. Holding the other half she painted the girl's lips with the red juice. She pulled away barely before tasting the juice on her lips. Her mouth came back to the morsel sucking the pulp from the skin then taking that also as her hand reached out for more. Finding me watching her, she stopped.

"Go ahead miss, take what you want, Savant brought plenty for the night."

She grabbed a cluster of the orbs, and began devouring them. Savant stopped her progress ever so often with a kiss, and to share one from between her breast. As we drank our Brandy, I fired a cigar and noticed how easy it was for Savant to take her share of the grapes without eating many at all. Using her charms, and body, to share what ever she took, getting the other two to eat the bulk. Watching her work explained to some degree how it was that her and Brite had coerced me so into doing whatever they wanted. But damn it, I have paid for someone to fuck this girl, so let's get on with it. Unbuttoning my britches and getting a hand full of hair "Narcissa, so you like putting orbs in your, mouth put these in there" slamming her face first into my crotch. She spilled a few grapes on the floor as the scent of my unwashed manhood enveloped her nostrils.

"Wash me with your tongue, or is that not lady like?"

A muffled groan came from my lap, and then two more from the other side of the carriage. Savant had driven two fingers in the whore's cunt, as she tried to suck all of the oxygen from her lungs. She pulled at the girls top till her small tits were visible. Gnashing at them with her sharp teeth in small pinches, Savant had the girl writhing, as she put another finger into her arse hole. The bitch's legs went out straight, as Savant worked her majik, but breathing was no easier for her. Savant had put a ribbon around the girls neck, and was choking her with it. As the whor's eyes rolled back, her body went into convulsions from the mightiest orgasm I had ever witnessed. Savant released the ribbon and dropped to the floor, licking up the inside of one thigh then the other, before two small hands were wrapped around the back of her head pulling her closer.

"Sir can we take this one home with us. I know that Hardwick would enjoy her being there," Savant asked lustily.

"Do you think that she would make it with him? You know how he is."

"I'll keep an eye on them. I would just like to have my sister back with me for a time."

"She's your sister?" I almost threw Narcissa to the floor at this revelation.

"Why yes, Sir. She can stay in my room. I don't use it much these days anyway. Please."

"Does Brite know about her?"

"She is the one that set it up for her to be in that doorway."

"But she doesn't look anything like you. How is she your sister, and why would you do that with her?"

"Our mother got around a bit, and when she brought men home with her we would entertain them while mother was busy. It made extra money."

"Okay okay okay, but she is your responsibility, do you understand me? And you, you will do as I say when

I say it, no matter what."

"Yes Sir, oh thank you thank you. You wont regret it."

"Well, if you are going to the house with us, both of you come over here." Pulling Narcissa up by the hair, "She is passed out, and I'm not done yet."

They helped me prop Narcissa in the corner before the small cunt wrapped herself around me for the ride and Savant sucked on my ballocks til cream oozed from her little sister.

1 may, 1888

ardwick looked confused as he came in the parlor looking for the gift that I had told him was there for him. Finding three girls sitting there, talking, one of which he had never seen before. He scanned the room in search of the present. Savant stood up as he came farther in the room and introduced him to her sister, Rose. Rose extended her hand to him, and curtsied. He bowed to her, as he took her hand, getting ready to kiss it, before she shook his.

"It's a pleasure to meet you Mr Hardwick. I've been told so much about you."

"I, umm, yes, it is a pleasure to meet you, too."

"How do you like your gift, Hardwick?" I asked.

"I have not found it yet, Sir."

We all laughed riotously, as Rose kissed him hard on the mouth.

"I suppose I'm your gift, Mr Hardwick."

"You are giving me a girl? What am I to do with a girl!"

"Anything you want as long as I'm not busy with her."

Dumbfounded he looked at each of us. "You cannot give someone another person."

Rose gripped his hand. "You can if they are willing to be a gift. Come let me show you what a good gift I can be."

He turned his head to us as it was a joke or something

as she led him out of the parlor and up the stairs. I did not see them the rest of the morning.

Savant came with me to the office so we could work in private. I am still not sure exactly how to make the tincture. One more lesson from her will instill it. Adding a few drops of opiate to the herbs Savant keeps with her will increase the speed of seduction I need to perform my task.

"Why do you need the tincture with four women at your beckon?"

"It is not your duty to ask why."

"But you can have whatever you want from any of us?"

"My affairs are mine, that's all you need to know."

"Okay, but I was only trying to understand your purpose."

"You would not understand, no matter how much you knew. Get the grapes I need to go out again tonight."

Giving her or anyone the nature of my quest before I find the cure would end the progress I now see. The cure for Elizabeth is all that matters, not what my concubine, or anyone else would want to know about it.

Howard is my trust, and I believe he would die for me if it became necessary. One day that may be challenged, but today he is my trusted driver. He was a sharp eyed shot in the military, and despite his age he can still hold himself against two or three men. Most want to bring a Blue Bottle with them when they go into the Chapel. I'll pick Howard over them all. He taught me how to use my stick and blade when we first met. Today I have all of them with me not to fear anything or person in this piss house. The whore sitting next to me has no understanding of her future. She thinks she has one. Tonight is her future: no beyond, no tomorrow, no heaven, only hell.

"Let us go home, Howard."

"Do you have what you need sir?"

"We will find out after we get in the basement. Now home, make it quick."

"Aye Captain."

2 May, 1888

The whore felt like a worn out feed bag. She was not useful to me for anything except to stoke the furnace, and fattening for the hog. The grapes worked incredibly, as she never moved even when cleaving through the grizzly whore. I will find one that will match my sweet Elizabeth.

Today I will take the girls with me to Trafalgar Square for a little outing a luncheon at the cafe perhaps. I'm sure some of the blue blood bastards from the club will be out and about. We will see what they think about us now. No more feeling sorry for us and our life.

"Ladies, get ready to go out. Your most outrageously seductive outfits will be on the button for today."

"Where are we going?" asked Narcissa.

"To Trafalgar for lunch on the square, and today you can act like anyone you want to be for the day as long as you swoon over me."

"This will be exciting." The sisters agreed in unison.

"What about Hardwick? Is he going, too?"

"Today he will assist Howard with the horses. This day is for us or shall I say me. We need to be there by noon, now go find your other self."

The girls lined up at the door in their tightest corsets and lowest cut dresses. A glorious line up of cleavage. They did well as they put on sparkling necklaces to direct the eyes even more. The sisters were right, this will be exciting.

Trafalgar was proud London's high achievement in Westminster, and we were going to stick a dagger through it's heart.

Howard pulled the carriage to the center of the square as Hardwick jumped from the back to set the step and open the door. All eyes were on us as I climbed out and helped the girls down, each one bending over slightly for a better view of their jewels. Standing there with them all around me for Howard to pull away, you could see people looking and talking about our appearance in this high area. We strolled arm in arm over to a table at the cafe, as others stopped to let us pass, talking to each other in hush tones. We were no longer the one of misfortune, with a wife laying in her box bed, her son by her side, but one to be envied by the lot of them. They will all know me. I will be the talk of the town. No the world. Everyone — will know my name.

The girls had fun with the boys that waited on us. Dropping their forks or kerchief when they were at the table. This constituted them either bending over as seductively as they could, while looking up at the poor imbeciles, or having him pick it up for them. Grabbing his hand, and holding it to their breast while telling him thank you. Needless to say we got more attention than all of the tables in the courtyard. They even forgot to charge us for our meal, and the breast were seasoned superbly. With a lift of my cane handle Howard pulled the carriage up for our departure. The owner of the cafe came out to hold the carriage door for the ladies. They all smiled at the portly man, giving him a big hug and kiss on the cheek as they disappeared into the box. I looked over his shoulder to see a woman standing in the doorway with a look of murder on her face. I shoved a pound note in his pocket and closed the door on him, and his demise.

3 May, 1888

Hardwick bounded down the steps two at a time racing his way to the kitchen.

On his return back past the door. "Should I ask what your hurry is young man?"

"Rose wants some tea this morning, and well you know, sir."

"Yes, my boy I know very well what a woman can do to or get you to do for them. Have fun."

"Thank you sir, I will sir, I mean."

"Yes, we all know what you mean."

The other two girls popped out from under the quilt I had covering my lap, and grinned at him. His upper body flushed red as he hurried away from all the eyes on him.

"Don't do anything we wouldn't" Savant shouted as he disappeared.

The jingling of cups on saucers became an ensemble, as his pace increased up the stairs.

Narcissa asked "Do you really think he knows as much as he thinks he does?"

"Not at all dear, but Rose does, and everything is about learning, now is it not? We never understand by only reading, but by putting those words into practice do they become clear. Now lay your head back down and rest my dear. You had a hard night" I chuckled.

"You are terribly bad, sir."

"So nice of you to notice. What do suggest we do about it?"

Savant perked up "I have a suggestion."

"Girl you always have a suggestion. Let me guess, we all retire back to my room?"

"And why should we not? Your schedule is clear for today. You up for some more fun Narcissa?"

"You two go without me."

"Oh come on, you know you want to, and I can feel that he wants you, too."

"Fine, then but can I sleep during it?"

"If you think you can but it's going to be harrrd again."

Savant pulled Narcissa to her feet and turned to me in all their glory. "Well, are you coming with us?"

"I will be up in a few minutes. I need to speak with Howard first."

"Well don't be too long, we may have to start without you" Savant said. Smacking Narcissa's creamy white arse, leaving a red hand print from the blow, the girls ran giggling up the stairs.

"Howard, have you checked the Hog pen this morning?"

"Yes sir. Nothing is left, and I tended the furnace all night as you asked."

"Good. Did everything burn like we wanted?"

"Some of the bones are still there, but I'm the only one that works it, sir. Are you wanting to go out again tonight?"

"Not tonight. I need to see if anything has been reported first. We will resume our hunt tomorrow."

"As you wish sir."

"Have you said anything to Margret about our excursions?"

"You asked me not to, but she has had some question about the extra meat in the icebox."

"And?"

"I told her that it was some special wild game you asked me to get for you, and she will need to age it before cooking."

"Very good, your confidence will be rewarded. Now, I have two other things to put to bed."

"Yes sir, I saw them passing me in the hall. Very nice if you don't mind me saying, sir."

"Yes they are, if you want to try one sometime let me know. I can arrange that for you without Margret finding out."

4 May, 1888

The station was quiet for a change as I walked back to Frederick's office. "How is my friend doing this morning? Has the tonic helped with the imminent doom that is your life?"

"What? Oh yes, come in. It's good to have you instead of all the ones that only want to tell me how worthless I, and the rest of the police force, are. Do you perchance have another bottle with you? The one you gave me last has been gone a few days now, and I have had to resort to other methods to cure these headaches."

"I gave you enough to last a normal person six months."

"You may have, but I'm not a normal person if you have not noticed."

"I have noticed that you self medicate in some less than respectable areas."

"You have no proof of that," Frederick growled.

"My dearest of friends, I don't need any because it is between us. Do you not remember that I was the one who came, and retrieved you from a den, so you would not be reduced in rank? Giving my apology for you being late for your shift? And shall I bring it up that you never even thanked me for saving your arse?"

"I know. Yes, you have helped me more than I could repay. Don't expect to hear this leave my mouth again, but Thank you."

"I never expected to hear it this time; although, it is welcome."

"What brought you here this morning anyway?"

"A friend is not welcome to just stop in for a cup and conversation?"

"Yes, but you never come here unless I send for you or you are working on something, and I did not send for you."

"Well yes, I was wanting to look back through some of your case files of missing people. To see if I missed anything on my reports to you. I have a free day and…"

"And you wanted to play inspector for a day? Hell, come on then, it cannot hurt to have another person looking through them. If anyone ask, I gave you permission, but nothing leaves the room."

The room was stacked with files. A lone table sat in the center with a hard back chair on each side. A single lamp hung overhead, illuminating the room which was mostly dark. My eyes slowly adjusted to the darkness as I worked at reading the dates on top of each stack. After about an hour I finally found the weekly report log I was looking for. Nothing. Not a single report from the Chapel was on it. Did no one care to report, or was it that they mistrusted the police so much, that they wouldn't talk to them about it? Either way, I had my answer. I decided waiting a while longer before going back to Frederick's office would be best.

"Sorry ole chap, but I didn't; couldn't find out anything more for you."

"It is a mess in there. We get so many that there is no room in the cabinets anymore."

"Yes I noticed that, lucky for me there were dates on top of each stack. Wish I could have been more help."

"Well you tried, if you think of anything else let me know. I need to get back to work. You can see your way out?"

"I will send you another bottle. We both know you will not come and pick it up."

He looked up from the papers he was reading and

nodded an affirmative.

"Howard, make ready for tonight. We will leave here at eleven for another trip."

The horses stomped at the ground, ready to get moving. They were not interested in waiting on me to board. The coach lights reflected in their globose eyes. A yellow red fire that seemed to be coming from deep inside, reflecting the demon that held their true spirit. Like the man with the knife enraged to action these beast were excited by the night, and its anticipation. Howard held firm to the reins even as their heads tossed. The box lurched forward, catching me hard in the shoulder.

"Sorry sir, these beast are wild tonight. Don't know what has gotten into them."

"Everything is fine Howard, try to hold them till I get seated if you can."

"Aye sir, doing me best."

"One second more. Now turn them loose. Head them toward the Chapel. Let them run for a tittle."

"Your pleasure, sir."

The woods creaked from the assault of stones battering the metals, as hoofs sparked a warning to any that dare mark their path. Careening around a corner the upper edge of the box scraped a post blowing out the lamp. The road narrowed to where only a push cart should travel, but the horses pulled forward, as rats scurried out from in front of them. One did not make it, as the box tilted, and bounced over two soft thuds. A woman wailed as she picked up the insignificant from the road. Howard drove on, as the noise died. My other mind asked us. "What type of mother would have a child out in the road at this hour?" It answered its own question, "No true mother." Howard, now reining the horses in, let me know that our destination was closing, and preparations needed to be done soon. The grapes on the table, ready. Brandy and wine out in the holder, ready. Cheese and bread set on the side bench, ready. Now all we needed is someone to share it with. Few were out in this area, a rap on the trap would get Howard's attention.

"Sir?"

"Take the next left. Let us see if we can find somewhere more suitable."

"But Sir, the streets, there will not be enough room to turn the coach around should we need to."

"We don't have that here."

"Aye, correct Sir. I will do as you ask."

He was correct, too. The streets turned into little more than alleyways barely over two meters wide. The horses felt trapped and lashed out at anyone that got too close. An older woman stepped out to meet the horses. Stopping them with a rise of her hand. Colors, and flashes of gold, waved all about her slightly rotund body, as she coddled them both. Then rubbing a hand down the neck and body of one as she passed it on her way to my window. Howard was astonished by her, as much as the horses were, sitting there mouth agape, wide eyed, wordless.

"Do you know why you travel here tonight?" She asked. "You are seeking for something extremely valuable." Her heavy Eastern European accent was undeniable, as were the indigo tattoos upon her doughy skin. "You need me to give you a reading, it wont cost you tonight doctor."

"I don't need a reading, madam."

"You need one more than you care to admit. Just let me hold something personal of yours for a moment, and I will tell you where you shall find what you search."

"If you are sure of what you say?" Reaching for my notebook, "I have my dip pen here. It is one of my most personal items. Will it do?"

"It will do perfectly." Setting it in her left hand, which already held an indigo eye in it's palm, with indigo rays emitting down each finger. The eye squinted, as she rotated the pen with her other hand, as if to get a closer look at the whole of it. As she was almost to speak, a double edge blade protruded between jagged teeth. Her mouth emitted nothing, but a gasp for air, and a trickle of blood from both corners. Jumping back, there stood Howard, holding her up from behind, as the pen rolled from the tips of fingers to the carriage floor. Grabbing the pen up while unlatching the door, Howard shoved the lifeless body through the opening.

"Why did you do that?"

"I've seen my share of her type, Sir. Before long you would have been her slave. She was already placing you into a trance. Did you not see what she did to the horses? Now she can help in the larder. We must get home now, Sir. There will be ones out looking for her, unkind ones, Sir. I've seen what they do to those that they find."

Howard was scared, and I saw him laugh at a full grown lion charging him during a safari in Africa. For whatever this meeting was, he did not want to be part of it. He had the horses moving again not fast, but getting vacant of this area none the less. A long loop around the north part of town before going back to the house. The hand laid open, as the eye blinked with each lamp we passed under, I knew what I must do.

Howard pulled the coach next to the smokehouse, so we could carry the limp body inside, before he retrieved his blade. Dumping the carcass on the heavy wood table to do his work, he looked the body over and tugged at the hilt of his dagger. Bone scrapping iron, as it unsheathed from the wrinkled flesh. Taking it straight to the basin to wash the dark slick sticky slime from it. Miraculously only a small amount of blood escaped the wound. Congealing almost as soon as it hit air. Did she have some type of unknown healing properties?

"What type of creature is this, Howard?"

"A queen is what she would be called by her sort. Not a real queen, but the leader of her tribe, full of dark stuff. Did you see all the markings on her?"

"I saw the eye in her hand. What other markings do you see?"

"That is only one, look here." He put the edge of his knife under her clothes and ripped them up the center, exposing hundreds of such symbols that covered her

191

body.

"What do they all mean?"

"I don't know, Sir. Only way to protect you now is to—" he gazed at one of them, "nevermind, Sir, I will take care of this one, you go on to bed. Get some rest, Sir. What had you handed her that the eye looked at, Sir?"

"My pen was all, but the eye seemed to keep looking at me, even when she laid dead in the coach."

"Leave it with me, Sir. It will be back in your study in the morning, but you will need to get another one to carry with you."

"My pen, why do you need that?"

"Nothing for you to fret about sir, but do as I say on this. Now give me the pen, Sir, and away with you. I have much work to do tonight."

Reaching the door to the house, the whack of a meat cleaver could be heard. I Stopped to look around. Where was the light coming from? A small beam from my bedroom was showing on the side yard. Easing the door to the mudroom let me peer through the kitchen door. I took off my shoes, so the leather would not slap on the hardwood floors. There was a low sound of music coming from upstairs. The landing proved me sort of right, as I heard one of the girls say "ride him like the little stud he is." Finding the door was no problem. My room was the only one with light emitting from it. There they are; Two empty bottles of wine, and a mostly drained bottle of Brandy, sat on the table; Hardwick nude, on all fours, with Rose sitting on top of him like lady Godiva, riding him around the room, Savant and Narcissa naked on the bed, swatting at his bare arse as he passed by them. I cleared my throat, helping Hardwick find himself, as Rose fell to the floor.

"Hardwick, go to your room. I will deal with you in the morn."

"But Sir, we were only—"

"I saw what you were doing. Now get your clothes and go to your room."

"Sir, let me explain—"

"I will not hear anymore from you tonight, do as I say, boy!"

A firm knuckle across the cheek helped him find his way. I would regret that later, but I was not going to be talked back to.

"You three want to play games; play them with me, not with the boy. You are here to teach him, not make him your puppet."

"We were only having some fun. Besides you were out. Can we ask who you have been out with, and why you carried her into the smokehouse with Howard?"

"No, you may not. Anyway, she is Howard's business now, and not a word to Margret. It has been a long day. Rose, get in bed. No not your bed girl, this one here, you will stay with us this night. It will be your job tonight to assure all are satisfied in this room. A job that I hope you are up to, my fancy is dark this eve. Now help me with my clothes."

5 May, 1888

Drink helps all women become more compliant to your wants. Waking with three naked women in bed with you attest to that. Today I will take them all for new dresses, as a reward. The spectacular appearance of them with me again, torches for the gossip's fire in the square.

They were all feeling the effects of last night. Rose a bit more than the others, but their day brightened with my new plans for today. Howard had left the pen in my study along with some curious items. The pen laid gently on the fingers of the old woman's hand along with an inkwell placed in the hollowed out pupal of the eye, in the center of its palm. Two lampshades were fashioned out of her tattooed flesh, and placed on the lamps that sat on each end of the desk. The runic symbols highlighted from the light behind had no meaning to me, but from his actions the night before they did to Howard. I left looking at the hand once more, before setting the bolt on the door.

My ladies are ready to go. It amazes me how fast they can get ready when we are going out to have fun and buy things. Hardwick stumbled out of his room, clutching his head, almost running into me. Not talking, or caring, about what we were going to do today, he just wanted us to leave and make it quiet again. I patted him on the shoulder.

"Have a bit too much drink last night?"

"My head hurts."

"It will for a while. But before you sit down in your miserable state I need you to go get a coach for me and the girls to take to the west side."

"Why not Howard? He can drive you."

"Howard was working for me all night. He needs to sleep."

"I need to sleep, too."

"You can, boy, but I need the coach first, then you can do whatever you please."

"Tis always what you need. You don't give a shit about what others need."

"My dear boy you have to understand. What I'm doing will shape your whole future. It may not seem to you that I have anyone else in mind when I do the things I do, but you are the one in this house that I care for the most. Now make haste and get me the cab, and I will not ask a thing from you the rest of the day."

He silently went out the door to the street, mumbling something that I'm quite positive that I didn't want to know. He will be a great man one day, if only I can shape him properly. A short time later the cab pulled up in front of the house with Hardwick sitting next to the driver. Climbing down from the carriage he walked past us without a word, even though Rose tried to give him a kiss as he went by.

"Ladies, he's not feeling well this morning, it will only dampen the spirits of all to bother him more."

"I only wanted to know if he had a good time last night," Rose said. "Maybe I can make him feel better when we get back?"

"You can see about him then. Now the West Side is calling us. Everyone in, let's go make people uncomfortable."

These three had made a bond that was undeniable. Two sisters, and an unlikely companion, that when put together mischief abound from them. It was a great joy watching how they played with, and off each other.

How they could make a person, man or woman, blush without trying. It was natural to them, a gift some would say. Me, myself, I just entertained the game, that fans the flames of gossip. After our first trip out together, they wore nothing that would obscure their charms, and they loved the attention granted to them. They drank, and had cigars in public, asking whomever is nearby to light them up, as they licked on the tip of the stick, before pinching off the end between their teeth. Women become infuriated, as the men with them fondled for a match.

The seamstress at the dress shop saw what they wore. She had trouble with their style, but the money was good, so they started working. Showing fabrics, taking measurements, and getting each girl's wants written down, they set to cutting and sewing as we went to eat. Promising us that the dresses would be done before close.

The feeling that we were being watched was a fact. The owner's wife of the cafe that we had eaten at before stood at the gate. Her glare of disdain with us coming towards the establishment was hilarious to me. When the girls saw her they pranced forward with more gusto, dancing past her, as hatred erupted from her eyes. When I got next to her, she turned on me.

"Sir, the last time you and your—ladies came here you failed to pay."

"Madam, I paid what I was asked to pay for."

"You will pay for everything before you leave today. My husband may think that it is fine for you to leave without paying, but I assure you sir, I don't."

"Whatever you think is appropriate, I will pay. We are not here to be vagabonds. We only want to engross ourselves in your fine food once again. It was so good last time, we were compelled to return. May I ask, are these your fabulously ambrosial dishes that are made here?"

"Why yes, Sir, they are. Is there some special item that you and the ladies were needing today? I can prepare other items that are not on the board if you would like."

"No, madam, what you have is wonderful, but I do have some special wild game that I'm presently smoking at the house. I would share some with you, to make amends for our last time here. That is if you would not take offense?"

"Fresh smoked game meat would be delightful, sir. Should I send someone for it?"

"No, as soon as it is ready, I will have my man drop it off to you. Would fifty be sufficient to settle?"

"That is too much, sir. Are you sure that you want to give us that much?"

"We can call it even, for last time, and this, if you would feel better about it."

The girls already had every type of food being brought out to the table when I got to them. The owner directed his attendants away from the table. He wanted to take care of their needs himself while he leered at my lovelies' attributes. Knowing that they were with me, he straightened up as I pulled out the chair.

"I'm sorry, Sir, I did not see you enter. Let me get you a draught to spice the tongue."

"Do you not have something a tittle harder my good man?"

"Yes Sir. What would you, I will bring you some of my best for your wait. I hope it will be satisfactory."

"What you bring will suffice. I am most sure."

His apology for not seeing me amused the girls.

After having their fun with the boys there, and feeding their egos, the girls were ready to take me wandering the square. Each one of them squeezed the owner and kissed his cheek as they left. I graciously kissed the matron's hand, and thanked her for the meal, as I left. The bill she was so demanded of when I arrived, had been forgotten. We left without paying again as she rushed to her husband, whispering in his ear. A wide grin enveloped by his cheeks appeared as he waved us a good day. She had told him our agreement.

We walked the square, waiting for the dresses to be

ready. The girls walked close to me but flirted with every man that passed. Chance had it, that several of the men from the Reform came our direction. Savant and Rose broke free and casually walked right through the middle of them, rubbing their finger tips along their low cut necklines as they passed. These better than thou solders of wealth could not contain themselves, as they fought to be the first to speak to me. I stopped to be pleasant, as the girls saddled up to me, giving the men what they wanted. A closer look at the beauty I surrounded myself with these days. The encounter would be recounted throughout the Reform many times before people would ask me about it. The seed was planted.

The old woman at the dress shop was waddling up to lock the door when it flung open and the girls flounced in.

"We are here to pick up the dresses," Narcissa announced in her most domineering tone.

"Well they are ready for you, madam," the old woman quipped back. "If your highness is ready we can get on with the fitting."

"You old trollop, you do understand we are your customers?"

"I don't care if you are the Queen, this is my home your in. Now do you want these new dresses," pointing toward the dress stands against the back wall, "or should I start making them into something respectable?"

We will enjoy this woman.

The dresses were each done to the girls' wants. A rich green with small pearls, and fine lace along the plunging front, for Savant. Rose picked a floral of roses, with small vines, and leaves making the shoulders, as to her namesake. Lastly, Narcissa's sat there in a raven color, with crystals sewn into the cloth all over the top. The girls ran to their perspective costumes as the shop girls put up dressing screens around each one. Rose emerged from behind her curtain first. The dress was immaculate on her, with a fall of the hem, from mid calf, to barely touching the floor in the back. The owner of the shop looked at them each disapprovingly, as they came out, but accepted the money without problem when the girls got redressed, adjusting and boxing the new dresses for us to carry home.

With a swirl of the cane the carriage pulled up into the center of the square, waiting for us to regress from the area. I needed to talk to Howard, and hurried the girls aboard while telling the driver to get us back to the house.

"Savant, go in and tell Howard to meet me in the smokehouse; it is imperative that I see him now." After paying the driver, I went around to the smokehouse and waited for Howard. The seconds ticked off, as did my restraint when Savant came out the kitchen door.

"Sir Howard will be a few minutes. I am afraid that He and Margret are a bit indisposed at the moment. I don't think they expected us back this soon, but I did tell him to meet you out here."

We went back in the Smokehouse to talk over this new event with ourselves.

"Well well, the old dog does still has some fire in him. Good for him. It will be worth the little extra wait to coax him for details." "What if he will not talk?" "Oh I can get him to talk, he always tells me things. Terrible awful thingies, he would never tell anyone, even Margret."

"Sir, you sent for me?"

"Welcome, old chap, now tell me how has your day been? A cigar to smoke after working hard?"

"Bless you sir, I have not had a good cigar in many a day." He stopped to light before continuing. "What can I tell you, sir? Working around the house on things that I've been neglecting recently."

"Really, and what have you been neglecting in my house?"

"Nothing sir, just some personal things."

"Personal? Personal! You know that nothing in this house is personal from me. Now tell me what you have been doing during my absents."

"To be honest with you sir…"

"Howard, no one is asking for honesty here. I know what you were doing. I just want to hear about how hard she wanted it, and how you dominated that old woman of yours. Lie to me man, that's what we do. Men are never honest about such affairs. You know the truth is too boring. So start over again, and let me hear what you have been doing today, and while you are at it, get that bottle of Brandy you have stashed out here. You know, the one you took from my liquor cabinet?"

And so I sat there listening to him tell me about all the things he wish he could do to her, and a few things that he probably did. You learn a lot about people when you get them talking about dreams, and fantasy, as if it were real. Even with all I know about Howard, this talk told me so much more. He was not that different from Hardwick in his darkness. I guess that is why I have kept him by my side these years. After he was done, I told him the reason I had asked him to join me out here, and what I needed from him. He informed me that the meat would be ready in a few more days. He had cut and packaged it where no one could tell its origin.

6 May, 1888

"This home is my sanctuary, we cannot keep bringing the dead to it."

"Why not? They are not looking for them here. Most have not even been reported as missing. What is the harm? You are beyond reproach, being the doctor for the police, and personal friends with the Inspector. He thinks you are trying to help him anyway."

"You only think with your edge, and the blood you can gather on it. You need to think of this sanctuary and all it offers the ones inside it, including yourself."

7 May, 1888

The child was so sweet as she collapsed in my arms, before he intruded on my mission. Such a waste of time he has taken from me. We had to bring them both back to the smokehouse. Not one, but two, back to our sanctuary. This must end soon.

The Blue Bottle lay naked on the block, waiting for his dispatch. His last dispatch from this side to the next.

"Oh my little piggy, why did you come squealing so loud? You understand that I had to commit you to my edge. With all the noise you were making, your brothers would soon have come to your aid. I do hope that your flesh is sweet, with just the right amount of fat, to take the heat. I will see first with your little head. Shall I boil it, roast it, or put it to the smoke? Peeling out those cheeks just to savor the meat. Plucking out an eye, like an oyster from its shell, oh what a fragrant smell. Those soft brains with my eggs in the morn, how lush you will be. You have caused me so much trouble, but have given so much of yourself for free."

10 November, 1888

Noise evaded the room as eyes jerked open to the quietness of the house. Howard's snoring could always be heard throughout the house at this time of night. Tonight, nothing.

In the darkness sat a box, perched on the table, across the room. Turning the knob at the base of the wall sconce let it blaze into life. The light immediately overtaking the darkness, eyes blinking, in submission to the sudden onslaught. Getting out of bed to examine closer, I found it to be a cold chest from the laboratory, used to keep specimens chilled for later study. Tied to the handle on top was a note written in red ink.

This should be what you need.

Mary said that she would have no use of it anymore.

Take care, my close friend,

Jack

Inside the chest was a full intact uterus. I prepared for the surgery without delay, going to Elizabeth's room with the chest. She lay in her bed unmoving, our son nested under her arm. Quickly I made the incisions to take out her dried up uterus, and replace it with the fresh one. I had read Mary Shelly's documentation on Victor's experiments, over and over again, these last two years. I had read of his remarkable success, but I have still failed my beloved. What will I tell her? How will she cope with being married to such a failure?

"There is the dark side in some that reeks of good. In the great, the darkness is buried in the core of being, let out in subtleness till needed. When the sight of terror reflects in their eyes. The terror from victims of past lives, so detached from earth and heaven. So many lives have I known, and will know. I find exuberance in the fear! A dramatic giddiness, as it oozes from victims. Finding themselves stranded and alone in the ocean of people. They ask the same. They pray the same. With me — they *die* the same."

"Who am I, you may ask? I am the dark of the night. The voice of your dreams. The scourge of police. The cape of kindness. The hand of forgiveness. The man in the black hat.

I Am The RIPPER."

So the Ending Begins

17 December, 1888

Elizabeth has quit talking to me. Her and my son have left me. The house is dead without them. My life here is finished.

Jack told me that when I'm ever in the United States look him up in New York.

I boarded a ship this afternoon, as the timbers glowed red on my past life, a plume visible from the ship's railing. The steam whistle shouted our departure as the ship pulled itself to deeper waters, and us toward a new home.

Good bye, London. Till we meet again,
Jack

18 December, 1888

London report of a gray matter. Yesterday a condemned home, once reported as the home of a prominent gynecologist of the East Side, went up in flames. Five bodies were found in the rubble: two men, three women, all presumed to of died in the fire. One of the men appears to be that of the Doctor — as his office has been closed since the death of his wife and child over two years prior in a failed delivery by the Doctor. None of the other bodies have been identified at this time. There was also discovery of human remains in the cellar furnace. Police are doing a full investigation on the scene.

Hello my lovely, Hello my sweetheart.
Can you see me in the dark?
When you walk alone in the park.
Will you remember the smell of my touch?
Will you know the touch of my breath?
Will you see the pulse of my life?
When you feel the blade of my knife.

Receipt Index

Roast Pigeon:

Pigeon, three quarter oz. Butter, Pepper and Salt to taste. Wipe the bird very dry, season them inside with pepper and salt, and put butter into the body of the bird; this makes it moist. Put it down to a bright fire, and baste well the whole time it is cooking (it will be done in twenty to thirty minutes); garnish with fried parsley.

Egg Sauce:

Four Eggs, half pint melted Butter (Sauce au Beurre), very little Lemon Juice. Boil the eggs till quite hard, which will be in about twenty minutes, and put them into cold water for half an hour. Strip off shell, chop the eggs into small pieces, not, however, too fine. Make the melted butter (Sauce au Beurre) 2oz. Butter, a dessertspoonful of flour, 1 quarter of a pint of water, salt to taste. Melt butter in a saucepan, add flour, and add the water very gradually with a seasoning of salt; stir it constantly till the whole of the ingredients are thoroughly blended and leave no lumps. Let it thoroughly boil, add eggs and lemon juice, when it is ready add a little cream and serve very hot.

Toast Points:

Cut as much bread as needed into one quarter inch slices. Toast on both sides in front of a bright fire, making sure not to blacken it and ruining the appearance or flavor. Cut butter into small pieces and place on hot toast, when just starting to melt spread evenly. Immediately cut into triangles and serve on hot plate.

Rib of Beef A La Bourgeoise

Select a three-rib piece from the thinnest end of the ribs; remove two of the bones, leaving the middle one only. Lard the lean part of meat with lardons of raw, salted, and unsmoked ham. Season with mignonette and allspice, wrap it up in bards of bacon and tie. Garnish the bottom

of a buttered braiziere, with sliced onions and a carrot, a garnished bunch of parsley, and moisten with one gill of Maderia wine, one gill of brandy, and a sufficient quantity of stock to immerse the meat to three quarters its height. Boil, skim, and let cook for two and a half to three hours, turning the meat over and basting it frequently; then remove it from the fire, and leave it in the stock to get about two-thirds cold, then take it out and lay it under a weight, and when completely cold pare it nicely into the shape of a cutlet; scrape the surface of the bone, and glaze the meat. Set it on a dish, and garnish around with pear-shaped carrots and turnips, previously blanched and cooked in white broth with a little sugar, and reduced to a glaze. Clarify the stock in the braiziere in order to make a jelly, garnish the dish with this jelly chopped up, and cut triangular-shaped croutons; fasten into the meat three handsome hatelets of vegetables; trim the bone with a large paper frill.
Charles Ranhofer 1862-1894

Oysters A La Hollandaise

Poach the oysters, then drain them, dress them into a deep dish and cover them with a Hollandaise sauce.

Eggs A La Bedford in Cocottes

Cover the bottoms and sides of a few cocottes with a layer of liver baking forcemeat, thickened with a little raw forcemeat thinned with duxelle sauce and Madeira wine; break a fresh egg over, season the white with salt and pour a little hot butter over the top. Place these cocottes in a sautoir containing a little hot water; poach the eggs for eight to ten minutes in a slack oven, and after removing bestrew with truffles and cooked beef tongue, cut either in small dice or chopped up; dress the cocottes on a dish.

Turkish Coffee

To be made with the same proportion of Java as Mocha, ground and passed through a very fine sieve. Pour ordinary black coffee in a coffee pot, as many cups as needed, and add for each cup a common coffeespoonful of coffee passed through a sieve, also a lump of sugar; stand it on the fire, boil for two minutes, then take it off and pour in a little cold water to settle the coffee; let stand again for a few minutes. Serve powdered sugar with the coffee.
Charles Ranhoffer 1862-1894

Queen Cakes

Ingredients - 1 lb. of flour, ½ lb. of butter, ½ lb. loaf sugar, 3 eggs, 1 teacupful of cream, ½ lb. Of currants, 1 teaspoonful of baking-powder, essence of lemon or almond to taste.
Work the butter to a cream; dredge in the flour, add the sugar and currants, and mix the ingredients well together.

Whisk the eggs, mix them with the cream and flavouring, and stir these to the flour, beat the paste well for ten minutes; add the baking-powder, put it into small buttered pans, and bake the cake from a quarter to half an hour. Grated lemon-rind may be substituted for the lemon and almond flavoring, which will make the cakes equally as nice.
Mrs. Beeton 1892

Blackthorne Cocktail

Fill mixing glass 2/3 full shaved ice. ¼ teaspoonful lemon juice. 1 teaspoonful syrup. ½ jigger vermouth. ½ jigger sloe gin. 1 dash bitters. Stir; strain into cocktail glass and serve.
Tom Bullock 1917

Meat and Vegetable Pie

Take either cold beef, veal, or mutton. Mince fine, and mix it with some bread crumbs; have a dish covered with paste, put some mince at the bottom, then put in a few bearded oysters, next the limbs of turkey, chicken, or rabbit boned; then put a layer of peas or spinach, some force meat balls, and a few small mushrooms, pour in some rich gravy, thicken with some cream and flour; strew it over thickly with bread crumbs, and at the top an egg beat well; then bake in the oven.
Mrs. Ella E Meyers 1876

Huîtres Marinées

Blanch some large oysters, drain them after the first boil and keep the liquor; boil some vinegar with cloves, whole pepper, whole allspice, half an ounce of each for every quart of vinegar, and add a little mace; put two-thirds of the oyster liquor with one third of the vinegar, and also the oysters into a hermetically closed glass bottles, and keep them in a cool place. Serve on side dishes with sliced lemon and sprigs of parsley set around.

Consomme Deslignac

Chicken Consomme thickened with tapioca, Garnished with dice of Royale, Roundels of stuffed lettuces a chervil shreds.

Cream d'Asperges

Bend some small green asparagus, beginning at the root end, so as to break it off, keeping only the tender parts (two pounds); cut into one inch length pieces, wash well changing the water several times, then drain and throw into boiling, salted water, continue the boiling for ten minutes, then drain. Put four ounces of butter into a saucepan; when very hot add the asparagus, and fry colorless on a quick fire; moisten with two quarts of broth, and when done, drain and smash through a fine sieve. Add one pint of veloute to the broth, color it with some spinach green or Breton vegetable coloring, season with salt, sugar and nutmeg, and just when serving thicken the soup with raw egg-yolks diluted in cream, and work in two ounces of butter. Serve separately some croutons souffles made with pate a chou rolled in strings and cut in three-sixteenth of an inch lengths; these pieces to be rolled in flour, then rolled around in a sieve to make them round. Fry in hot fat; or asparagus tops may be served as a garnishing instead of the croutons.

Timbales a la Mentana

The salpicon to be made of chicken livers a la Duxelle, thickened with egg-yolks, to be used when cold. Butter some timbale molds, and place on the bottom a one inch in diameter slice of truffle, cut away the center with a three-quarters of an inch vegetable cutter, and replace the truffle by a piece of red beef tongue. Decorate the sides of the mold with thin, eighth of an inch wide strips of tongue. Laid on slanting, having ten strips in all, and in the center between every one, a round bit of truffle measuring three-sixteenths of an inch across, with a smaller one one-eighth of an inch on the top and bottom, also laid on slanting, making three round bits of truffle between the two strips of tongue. Fill the insides and bottom with a chicken and cream forcemeat, and in the center lay a ball of the prepared salpicon; then more forcemeat, and poach. Invert on a dish containing a little consomme and serve separately a perigueux and tomato sauce mixed.

For salpicon of chicken livers a la Duxelle, cut some chicken livers in quarter inch squares; fry them in butter with a little shallot, mushroom, and truffles, all chopped finely, and mingle with a little well reduced half-glaze.

Salmon sauce Crevettes

Pound one ounce of salmon coral with a little vegetal carmine, a teaspoonful of English mustard, some salt, cayenne pepper, and the juice of two lemons; pass all this through a fine sieve, and mix in with it slowly a pint of mayonnaise sauce. Cook shrimp in court-bouillion, serve with parsley sprigs and Salmon Mayonnaise.

Pommes a l'Anglaise

Peal potatoes and cut into oblong finger shape 1.5 to 2 inches long rinse, drain, place in sauce pan and cover with cold unsalted water. Bring rapidly to the boil. Drain the potatoes. Heat a knob of butter and a little oil in a saute pan big enough to hold the potatoes in a single layer. As soon as the fat is hot add the potatoes, seal them over a brisk heat, then saute them gently for about 15 minutes. Cover and place in a preheated oven (200 degree C, 400 F) and continue cooking for about 10 minutes. Remove from oven as soon as they have browned. Drain and season with fine salt. Coat eight fillets of cod with egg and breadcrumbs and cook them in clarified butter. Arrange on a long plate and cover with maitre d'hotel butter. Serve with potatoes around edge sprinkled with chopped parsley.

Felet de boeuf a la Chevrelat

Trim carefully a tenderloin of beef, remove all the fat and nerves, then cut it into slices each one weighing five ounces; beat them lightly to have them all of the same thickness, then pare and cut them into round shapes. Salt on both sides, dip the in melted butter or sweet oil, and broil on a moderate, well sustained fire; they should take six minutes for rare, eight minutes for medium and ten for well done. When half cooked turn them over and finish the other side. cover the bottom of a hot dish with bearnaise sauce, sprinkle over with chopped parsley, lay the minions on top, and on each one set an artichoke bottom slightly smaller than the minion, and previously cooked and sauted in butter. Garnish with a little macedoine thickened with veloute and fine butter, and season well.

Tomates Farcies

Cut off tops half an inch in diameter, and scoop out the interiors; squeeze them without misshaping them, and remove the insides with a small vegetable scoop. Rub lightly the bottom of a bowl with some garlic, and for half a pound of chicken forcemeat placed in a bowl, mix in the same quantity of foies-gras taken from a terrine; add a quarter a pound of mushrooms and two ounces of chopped truffles, salt, pepper, nutmeg, chopped parsley, a little Madeira wine, and grated parmesan cheese. Fill the tomatoes with this preparation and bake them in a moderate oven for twenty minutes.

Chapons a la Lyonnaise

Take a long thin French loaf and cut the crust off of it and let harden for twenty four hours, then rub with a garlic clove, and sprinkle with a little olive oil. Chop some onion and glaze in butter till golden, dress bread with onions, deglaze pan with a little vinegar and use this to finish off bread, sprinkle with chopped parsley and serve.

Petets Pois au Beurre

Put one pint of fresh shelled green peas into a saucepan with a little cold water, stirring in a piece of butter; add salt, bring to boil and cook with lid on. When sufficiently done and liquid reduced add a small piece of kneaded butter; then take from the fire and finish by incorporating a large piece of butter divided in small bits. The peas should be well buttered and thickened so that the liquid be entirely absorbed.

Croquettes de Homard a la Victoria

Cut a pound of Lobster into dice shapes, and have also one-quarter pound of truffles cut the same size as the lobster. Put a quart of veloute, into a sautoire, season with salt, white, and red pepper, and add half a pint of celery puree, let reduce and moisten with cream; and incorporate into two ounces of lobster butter for each pound; then add the lobster, let this preparation get quite cold, then divide into balls an inch and a half in diameter, forming these into cork shaped croquettes, two inches in length, roll them in beaten egg and then bread-crumbs, and fry a fine color; dress on folded napkins, arranging a bunch of fried parsley on top.

Sorbet Regence

Sorbet made with lemon and champagne.

Becassines Bardees

Snipe wrapped in bacon and tied with string then roasted in butter in a pan for five minutes.

Salade de Laitue

Wash and dry lettuce, shred up finely; season and lay in a salad bowl, cover with a mayonnaise sauce. Serve garnished with hard boiled eggs and plenty of herbs.

Entremets De Douceur-Biscuits, Frascati

Break twelve eggs, putting the yolks in one vessel and the whites in another; add to the yolks three-quarters of a pound of powdered sugar and a quarter of a pound of vanilla sugar and beat well with a whip to obtain a very light and frothy preparation. Then add to it six ounces of flour and six ounces of fecula sifted together, and afterward the stiffly beaten egg-whites; stir the preparation until perfect. Butter and flour a plain cylindrical mold; fill it two-thirds full with the preparation and cook it in a slack oven. As soon as done unmold and let get cold. When cold, cut it up in transversal slices a quarter of an inch thick and cover each slice with a layer of fine vanilla cream; dredge the surfaces with a finely chopped salpicon of pineapple and pistachios. Reconstruct the biscuit to its original shape, cover it with a layer of apricot marmalade and bestrew the sides with chopped pistachios. Now place it on a dish; decorate the top with a rosette of fine candied pink and white pears cut in four and intermingle them with lozenges of angelica: brush these fruits over with a very thick syrup and surround the base with a row of apples cooked in butter, having small sticks of angelica placed between each. Fill the hollow center of the biscuit with cream rice flavored with vanilla and keep the biscuit warm for twenty minutes, serving it with a flavored English cream sauce.

English Cream Sauce Flavored With Vanilla

Place in a vessel eight egg-yolks, half a pound of sugar and one ounce of starch; beat up a moment to have the mixture smooth. Stand a quart of milk on the fire in a saucepan with a split vanilla bean added to it and let boil; as soon as this occurs pour it gently over the eggs and stir all well together. Pour it all back into the saucepan, place it again on the fire and thicken the sauce without permitting it to boil, stirring continuously with a spatula, then strain through a fine sieve. The vanilla can be replaced by liquors added at the last moment.

Savarin aux Cerises

2 eggs, 60g sugar, 150ml milk, 50ml oil, 75g flour, 2 tsp yeast, 1 pinch salt, cherries.

Preheat oven to 210 □ In a bowl, mix the eggs with the sugar and add all other ingredients. Have the cherries in a cake pan, pour the mixture over, and bake for 30 minutes.

Glaces Napolitaine
Pack in a freezer a Neapolitan mold. It must be made in three divisions; fill one of the round parts with vanilla ice cream, the other with pistachio ice cream, and the flat one with strawberry water ice, having the mold quite full so that when forcibly closed the surplus cream runs out all around, thus preventing the ice from being salty; pack it well inice and let freeze for one hour; unmold on a small board and cut into five-eighths of an inch slices with a special tinned copper or silver plated knife so as not to blacken the ice; this knife should be dipped into warm water every time a slice is cut. Dress these slices on small lace papers.

Fruits – Aiglon

Peaches, Apricots, Nectarines - Poached in syrup dressed on Vanilla ice. Sprinkle with crystallised violets veiled with spun sugar.

Petits fours

These may be made of any sweet paste, pound or sponge cake, and allow of an endless variety of decoration, with different icings, crystallised fruits, candied peel, &c. The simplest way of making them is to cut pound or sponge-cakes into pretty, fanciful shapes, icing them with different colored icings, garnishing them, before the icing has set, with crystallised fruit, cut in fine slices, angelica, almonds, preserved cherries, and the like.

Mutton Cutlets with Mashed Potatoes

Ingredients - About 3 lbs. Of the best end of the neck of mutton, salt and pepper to taste, mashed potatoes.

Mode - Procure a well-hung neck of mutton, saw off about 3 inches of the top of the bones, and cut the cutlets of a moderate thickness. Shape them by chopping off the thick part of the chine bone; beat them flat with a cutlet-chopper, and scrape quite clean a portion of the top of the bone. Broil them over a nice clear fire for about 7 or 8 minutes, and turn them frequently. Have ready some smoothly-mashed potatoes; make a mound of them in a dish; pepper and salt the cutlets,and put them round the thick end downwards.

Beeton 1892

Scotch Rare-Bit

Ingredients - A few slices of rich cheese, toast, mustard, and pepper. Mode - Cut some nice rich sound cheese into rather thin slices; melt it in a cheese-toaster on a hot plate, or over steam, and, when melted, add a small quantity of mixed mustard and a seasoning of pepper; stir the cheese until it is completely dissolved, then brown it before the fire, or with a salamander. Fill the bottom of the cheese-toaster with hot water, and serve with dry or buttered toasts, whichever may be preferred. A small quantity of porter, or port wine, is sometimes mixed with the cheese; and, if not very rich, a few pieces of butter may be mixed with it to great advantage.

Overturned Eggs

Ingredients - Eggs, bread-crumbs, butter. Mode - Butter well some pretty little patty-pans, sprinkle them with raspings or finely-crumbed bread-crumbs. Break as carefully as possible an egg into each patty-pan, bake them on a hot plate, or with under heat only. Let the whites of the eggs set, then turn them out, bottom upwards, on spinach or ragout.

Tomato Soup

Ingredients – 1 quart of stock, 1 oz. Of butter, 12 tomatoes, 1 onion, 2 tablespoonfuls of crushed tapioca, pepper and salt.

Melt the butter in a stewpan, add the tomatoes and onions, sliced, cover with the lid and simmer on fire ten minutes; add the stock and seasoning; then boil gently until the tomatoes are well cooked; pass through a hair sieve. Return the soup to the stewpan, sprinkle in the tapioca, and boil until the tapioca is transparent. A tin of tomatoes will serve.
Mrs. Beeton 1892

Blackbird Pie

Stuff the birds with the crumb of a French roll soaked in a little milk, which put in a stewpan with 1-1/2 ounces of butter, a chopped shalot, some parsley, pepper, salt, a grate of nutmeg, and the yolks of two small eggs. Stir over the fire till it becomes a thick paste, and fill the insides of the birds with it. Line the bottom of the pie-dish with fried collops of rump steak, and place the birds on them neatly. Add four hardboiled yolks of eggs, and pour gravy all over, cover with puff paste, and bake for one hour and a quarter.
DRESSED GAME AND POULTRY: by MRS DE SALIS 1888

Fried Ham and Eggs

Ingredients – Ham ; Eggs

Mode - Cut the ham into slices taking care that they are the same thickness in every part. Cut off the rind, and if the ham should be particularly hard and salt, it will be found an improvement to soak it for about ten minutes in hot water, and then dry it in a cloth. Put it in a cold frying-pan, set it over the fire, and turn the slices three or four times whilst they are cooking. When done, place them on a dish, which should be kept hot in front of the fire during the time the eggs are being poached. Poach the eggs, slip them on to the slices of ham and serve quickly.
Mrs. Beeton 1892

Waffles, With Yeast

Sweet milk 2 cups; flour, 2 cups; yeast, 3 table-spnonfuls; 2 eggs; melted butter, 1 table-spoonful; salt, 1 salt-spoonful.
Directions – Set the sponge over night; in the morning beat and stir in the eggs and butter; bake in waffle-irons.

Dr Chase 1887

Compote of Gooseberries

Ingredients – to a pint of syrup allow nearly a quart of gooseberries.

Mode - Top and tail the gooseberries, which should not be very ripe, and pour over them some boiling water; then take them out, and plunge them into cold water, with which has been mixed a tablespoonful of vinegar, which will assist to keep the fruit a good colour. Make a pint of syrup and when it boils, drain the gooseberries and put them in; simmer them gently until the fruit is nicely pulped and tender, without being broken; then dish the gooseberries on a glass dish, boil the syrup for two or three minutes, pour over the gooseberries, and serve cold.
Mrs. Beeton 1892

Eggs-in-the-Nest

A nice dish for breakfast or tea. - Beat to a froth the whites of 6 eggs; a little pepper and salt; pour into a buttered baking tin, dip upon it6 table-spoonfuls of nice cream, 1 only in a place; upon each spoonful of cream drop 1 of the yolks whole (being careful not to break them); place in a moderately hot oven to cook and serve hot, as omelet should be.
Dr. Chase 1887

Roebuck Fillets a la Lorenzo

Pare two minion fillets of roebuck; suppress the superficial skin covering them and marinate for five or six hours in a little cooked marinade, drain, lard the entire upper surface with lardons, range them on a small buttered baking pan, one beside the other, cover with buttered paper and cook in a moderate oven for half an hour, until well done. Remove and cut them into slightly bias slices, and dress either in a straight row or else in a circle, and fill the sides or inside with braised chestnuts, stuffed Spanish olives, mushroom heads, round, medium truffles and large capers; cover with Pignola Italian sauce and game glaze and trim around with potato croquettes.
Charles Ranhoffer 1893

Apple Cheesecakes

Ingredients - ½ lb. Of apple-pulp, ¼ lb. Of sifted sugar, ¼ lb. Of butter, 4 eggs, the rind and juice of 1 lemon.

Mode - Pare, core and boil sufficient apples to make half a pound, when cooked; add to these the sugar, the butter, which should be melted, the eggs, leaving out 2 of the whites, and the grated rind and juice of 1 lemon; stir the mixture well; line some patty-pans with puff-paste, put in the mixture and bake about 20 minutes.

Mrs. Beeton 1892

Cheese Omelet

Beat up the eggs and add to them a tablespoonful of grated Parmesan cheese; add a little more cheese before folding, and turn out on a hot dish. Grate a little cheese over it before serving. The omelet made of three eggs is the one recommended for beginners. Break the eggs separately; put them into a bowl, and whisk them thoroughly with a fork. (The longer they are beaten, the lighter will be the omelet.) Add a teaspoonful of milk, and beat up with the eggs; beat until the last moment before pouring into the pan, which should be over a hot fire. As soon as the omelet sets, remove the pan from the hottest part of the fire, slip a knife under it to prevent sticking to the pan; when the centre is almost firm, slant the pan; work the omelet in shape to fold easily and neatly; and, when slightly browned, hold a platter against the edge of the pan, and deftly turn it out upon the hot dish. Salt _mixed_ with the eggs prevents them from rising, and when used the omelet will look flabby; yet without salt it will taste insipid. Add a little salt to it just before folding it and turning out on the dish.

Chicken Croquettes

Cut up the white meat of one cold boiled chicken, and pound it to a paste with a large boiled sweetbread, freed from sinews; add salt and pepper. Beat up one egg with a teaspoonful of flour and a wine-glassful of rich cream. Mix all together; put it in a pan, and simmer just enough to absorb part of the moisture, _stirring all the time_; turn it out on a flat dish, and place in ice-box to become cold and firm; then roll it into small neat cones; dip them in beaten eggs; roll in finely powdered bread crumbs; drop them in boiling fat, and fry a delicate brown. Handle them carefully.
* Thomas J. Murrey 1885

Squabs

Squabs are very nice broiled, but are at their best served as follows;—Select a pair of plump birds; clean them, cut off the legs, and remove the heads without breaking or tearing the neck skin; insert the forefinger in it, and separate the skin over the breast from the flesh; fill this with a nicely-seasoned bread stuffing, and fasten the loose end of the neck to the back. Place a thin wide slice of bacon over the breast, and fasten the ends with wooden toothpicks; put them in a pan; dredge with a little flour, and bake to a delicate brown; serve with fresh green peas.

BREAKFAST DAINTIES * Thomas J. Murrey 1885

Egg Balls.

Boil four eggs for ten minutes, and put them into cold water; when they are quite cold, put the yelks into a mortar with the yelk of a raw egg, a tea-spoonful of flour, same of chopped parsley, as much salt as will lie on a shilling, and a little black pepper, or Cayenne; rub them well together, roll them into small balls (as they swell in boiling); boil them a couple of minutes.

Rump-Steak Pie

Cut three pounds of rump-steak (that has been kept till tender) into pieces half as big as your hand, trim off all the skin, sinews, and every part which has not indisputable pretensions to be eaten, and beat them with a chopper: chop very fine half a dozen eschalots, and add them to half an ounce of pepper and salt mixed; strew some of the mixture at the bottom of the dish, then a layer of steak, then some more of the mixture, and so on till the dish is full; add half a gill of mushroom catchup, and the same quantity of gravy, or red wine; cover it and bake it two hours.
William Kitchiner 1775 - 1827

Mead

Ingredients for a six gallon cask: 24 lb. Of honey, 1 oz. Of hops, and ¾ oz. Of coriander-seed, the rinds of 3 or 4 oranges and lemons, 1 pint of brandy, and 6 gallons of water.

Mode; Set the water to boil; when quite hot work in the honey, and let it boil half an hour. While boiling, sew up the hops in a muslin bag and the coriander-seed, with the orange and lemon peels in another muslin bag, and put them into the liquor. Take off the scum as it rises, let the liquor stand twenty-four hours, then put it into the cask with the brandy; put the bung in lightly till fermentation is over, then bung the cask down quite close. It will be ready for use in nine or ten months; but if kept for a longer period it will be more mellowed, and the sweetness will go off. When the cask is tapped, the whole should be bottled, as it does not keep well on draught.

Corned Beef

Ingredients: 2 quarts water, 1 cup kosher salt, 1/2 cup brown sugar, 1 level teaspoons Pink Curing salt or Prague powder #1, 1 cinnamon stick, broken into several pieces, 1 teaspoon mustard seeds, 1 teaspoon black peppercorns, 8 whole cloves, 8 whole allspice berries, 12 whole juniper berries, 2 bay leaves, crumbled, 1/2 teaspoon ground ginger, 2 pounds ice, 1 (4 to 5 pound) beef brisket, trimmed.

Mode: Boil water, add salt, brown sugar, and saltpeter, stir to dissolve. Add the spices and let cool. Place brisket in a large crock. Pour marinade over meat. Meat should be submerged; use a weighted jar to hold meat under pickling solution. Refrigerate or set in a cool place for 10 days. After 10 days, remove from the brine and rinse well under cool water. Place the brisket into a pot just large enough to hold the meat, and cover with water by 1-inch. Set over high heat and bring to a boil. Reduce the heat to low, cover and gently simmer for 2 1/2 to 3 hours or until the meat is fork tender.

Sauer-kraut

25 lbs cabbage, 3/4 cup canning or pickling salt

Quality: For the best sauerkraut, use firm heads of fresh cabbage. Shred cabbage and start kraut between 24 and 48 hours after harvest. About 9 quarts Procedure: work with about 5 pounds of cabbage at a time. Discard outer leaves. Rinse heads under cold running water and drain. Cut heads in quarters and remove cores. Shred or slice to a thickness of a quarter. Put cabbage in a suitable fermentation container and add 3 tablespoons of salt. Mix thoroughly, using clean hands. Pack firmly until salt draws juices from cabbage. Repeat shredding, salting, and packing until all cabbage is in the container. Be sure it is deep enough so that its rim is at least 4 or 5 inches above the cabbage. If juice does not cover cabbage, add boiled and cooled brine (1-1/2 tablespoons of salt per quart of water). Add plate and weights; cover container with a clean bath towel. Store at 70 degrees to 75 degrees F while fermenting. At temperatures between 70 degrees and 75 degrees F., kraut will be fully fermented in about 3 to 4 weeks; At 60 degrees to 65 degrees F, fermentation may take 5 to 6 weeks. At temperatures lower than 60 degrees F, kraut may not ferment. Above 75 degrees F, kraut may become soft. If you weigh the cabbage down with a brine-filled bag, do not disturb the crock until normal fermentation is completed (when bubbling ceases). If you use jars as weight, you will have to check the kraut 2 to 3 times each week and remove scum if it forms. Fully fermented kraut may be kept tightly covered in the refrigerator for several months or it may be canned as follows: Hot Pack—Bring kraut and liquid slowly to a boil in a large kettle, stirring frequently. Remove from heat and fill jars rather firmly with kraut and juices, leaving 1/2-inch headspace. Adjust lids. Process pints 10 minutes and quarts 15 minutes in the boiling water canner. Raw Pack — Fill jars firmly with kraut and cover with juices, leaving ½ -inch headspace. Adjust lids. Process pints 20 minutes and quarts 25 minutes in the boiling water canner.

Hominy Porridge

Ingredients - Hominy, water, a piece of butter.

Mode - Pour boiling water on the hominy over night, and let it stand till morning. Then add more water if necessary, and boil it for at least half an hour. Stir in the butter just before serving.
Mrs. Beeton 1892

Egg Fritters

Ingredients - 3 oz. Of flour, 3 eggs, 1/2 pint milk

Mode - Mix the flour to a smooth batter with a small quantity of the milk; stir in the eggs, which should be well whisked, and then the remainder of the milk; beat the whole to a perfect smooth batter, and should it found not quite thin enough, add 2 to 3 tablespoonfuls more milk. Have ready a frying-pan with plenty of boiling lard in it: drop in rather more than a tablespoonful at a time of the batter, and fry the fritters a nice brown, turning them when sufficiently cooked on one side. Drain them well from the greasy moisture by placing them upon a piece of blotting-paper before the fire; dish them on a white d'oyley, sprinkle over them sifted sugar, and send to the table with them a cut lemon and plenty of pounded sugar.

Beef Pie

Ingredients — 2 lbs. Of tinned meet, 1/4 pint of stock, pepper, salt, 1 teaspoonful of mushroom catsup, 3 lbs. Of potatoes, flour.

Mode — Boil the potatoes, then mash them, Or use any cold potatoes for this dish. Cut the meat into neat pieces, roll or dredge them with the flour, then put in the stock and seasoning, and cover with the mashed potatoes. Bake half-an-hour in a good oven
Mrs. Beeton 1892

Fried Cutlets in White Wine Sauce

Ingredients – 6 lamb cutlets, salt and pepper to taste, 1 ½ ozs. Butter, 1 teaspoonful meat glaze, 1 tablespoonful white wine, 1 teaspoonful lemon juice, ½ teaspoonful chopped chervil or terragon

trim cutlets neatly and season or both sides with salt and pepper. Melt butter in a frying pan and fry cutlets lightly on both sides. When ready, serve in a circle or oval on a hot dish. Strain off butter. Add glaze and wine, lemon juce, herbs and a large pat of extra butter. Heat and pour over cutlets. Garnish with fresh scallions.

Stewed Stuffed Squab

Make some forcemeat balls, one for each bird required, of grated breadcrumbs, beef suet, sprinkled with flour and shredded cheese, a little chopped bacon and thyme, grated lemon peel, marjoram and parsley to taste. Moisten with a little melted butter and the yolks of two eggs and shape into balls. Put one in each bird. Tie birds up closely, and fry in butter till almost brown enough, then stew a little while in made gravy and white wine, thickening gravy before serving with a roux, and sharpening with lemon juice.

Laudanum Tonic

Ingredients – Oil of cloves, cinnamon, anise and peppermint, each 45 drops; Laudanum and ether 1 oz.; alcohol, 3 ozs.

Dose – A teaspoonful in 2 tablespoonfuls of sweetened water, and for an adult it may be repeated in 5 minutes to ½ hour, or 1 hour, according to the severity of the pain.

Collard Pig's Face

Ingredients – 1 Pig's face; salt.

For brine, 1 gallon of spring water, 1 lb. Of common salt, ½ handful of chopped juniper berries, 6 bruised cloves, 2 bay-leaves, a few sprigs of thyme, basil, sage, ¼ oz. Of saltpetre.

For forcemeat, ½ lb. of ham, ½ lb. of bacon, 1 teaspoonful of mixed spices, pepper to taste, ¼ lb. Of lard, 1 tablespoonful of minced parsley,6 young onions.

Mode – Singe the head carefully, bone it without breaking the skin, and rub it well with salt. Make the brine by boiling the above ingredients for a quarter of an hour, letting it stand to cool. When cold, pour it over the head, and let it steep in this for 10 days, turning and rubbing it often. Then wipe, drain, and dry it. For the forcemeat, pound the ham and bacon very finely, and mix with these the remaining

ingredients, taking care that the whole is thoroughly incorporated. Spread this equally over the head, roll it tightly in a cloth, and bind it securely with broad tape. Put it into a saucepan with a few meat trimmings, and cover it with stock, let it simmer gently for 4 hours, and be particular that it does not stop boiling the whole time. When quite tender, take it up, put it between two dishes and a heavy weight on top, and when cold, remove the cloth and tape. It should be sent to the table on a napkin, or garnished with a piece of deep white paper, with a ruche at the top.
Mrs. Beeton

Pig's Head Cheese

Ingredients – 1 Pig's head, 1 tablespoonful salt, pepper to taste, 1 tablespoonful sweet herbs

Boil a Pig's head in enough to cover it till the meat falls off the bones. Lift it out, remove meat from bones, and chop small season with salt, pepper and herbs to taste. Mix well, then place meat in a colander lined with a linen cloth. Press with a weight on top and turn out when cold.

Scrambled Eggs with Pig's Brain

Slice and braise a pig's brain then put to side to cool; cut it up into quarter inch squares and warm in butter. Prepare some scrambled eggs and when nearly done add the brains and mix them with the eggs. Dress in the center of a dish, pour around a little half-glaze sauce and surround with half-heart croutons of bread fried in butter.

About the Author

Daniel Dark, a native of Nashville, Tennessee, grew up with homicide every day. Having a homicide detective as a father, he was able to learn about those that were brought to justice, and the ones that were not.

Spending many hours in Central police headquarters and in his grandfathers hematology lab gave Daniel an unusual childhood and a love for science. Along with this, his great uncle owned the oldest book store in Nashville. His parents took him there regularly, where he developed a love of reading and found out about history.

Daniel went on to become an Electrical Engineer and Industrial Maintenance Manager till NAFTA took away his job. A year later he went to culinary school and studied Victorian cooking, after which he opened a Victorian-style restaurant.

He became a heart attack and stroke survivor at fifty years old, where he used writing to rehabilitate his brain. The first book written by Daniel was on Victorian Catsup, which had over two hundred catsup recipes in it from the late 1700's to 1910, with over sixty different flavors. Daniel used the book to start his 1876 Catsup company as Mr Catsup.

Knife's Tell represents his debut novel as an author.